The Lovable Rogue
Mysteries

David Biagini

DEDICATION

To all of those who made San Francisco the "Baghdad By The Bay." And to the memory of my mother, Rita.

ACKNOWLEDGMENTS

Thank you to Calvin Austin for helping make this book possible.

lovable rogue (luv-ă-bĕl rohg) *n.* 1. Charming, charismatic, and mischievous. 2. Willing to break the law to uphold the gentleman's code of conduct. 3. Impeccably dressed with excellent manners. 4. Comfortable with being out of step with the times. 5. Helps the underdog.

1 PROLOGUE

It was called it the "decade of greed". I called it the "decade of style." It was the 1980s, a time of ugly excess and undisciplined capitalism, of avaricious acquisitions and unrepentant cupidity. But it was also a return to dressing for dinner, single-malt scotches, and a general embracing of *le bon vie*.

As the decade unfolded, I found myself embracing *le bon vie* in San Francisco, then a glimmering jewel set in the cast of the Pacific Ocean, a city filled with character and characters, pretenses and pretensions, humor and humanity. Well, at times it fell short of humanity. But that's where I came in.

2 THE LOVABLE ROGUE

Style, you either have it, or you don't, and if you have it, you have it all the time. It doesn't matter what you're doing or where you are; if you have style, you have style. It's as simple as that. Take horse racing, for example. While many punters wear gym shoes and dungarees to the track, I typically attend in nothing less than an impeccably tailored double-breasted suit accented with a foulard tie made of Italian silk so smooth you could skate on it. If I'm feeling particularly sporting, I'll replace the foulard with one of Milan's more adventurous cravats. The deciding factor is always the stature of the track. The more elegant the venue, the more conservative my attire.

Today I was at Golden Gate Fields and was dressed rather sportingly in a double-breasted blue blazer, pale blue shirt with university striped tie, off-white cotton slacks, ultra-soft brown loafers, all topped off with a light gray fedora. That should tell you something about the stature of the track.

Golden Gate Fields is not the most glamorous place to view equestrian competition. It's not a dump, but it's not Churchill Downs. The people are urban, not urbane, the grass mowed, not manicured. It's a pure venue for horse racing, an aging track next to the San Francisco Bay on a piece of land real estate developers would kill for. My bet is one day, they will.

My other bet was on the long shot of the final race. She was a scraggly hag named MayBell that looked like the kind of horse that was once used to pull milk carts. But I had reliable information that she was faster than she looked.

The class of the field was Family Affair, the sure-thing favorite the pundits thought might be good enough for the Kentucky Derby. High expectations, indeed! He certainly oozed the arrogance that gives winning racehorses their championship looks. But oozing arrogance was not good enough for me. No, a good tip was much better.

The horses were led to the starting gate. When the bell rang, nine thoroughbreds kicked up clumps of grass as they sprinted forward. Family Affair fell back to fourth while MayBell made an impressive start and ran between the two front runners. After three furlongs, Family Affair passed MayBell and was nearing the lead. By four furlongs, Family Affair was second and making it look easy. MayBell remained in fourth. Had my tip been a dud?

Family Affair took the lead at the fifth furlong. If MayBell was going to make a move, now was the time to do it. But she remained in fourth place. Family Affair began to pull away from the field. I guess he was the favorite for a reason.

Things looked bleak for MayBell at the sixth furlong, but suddenly she bolted forward as if she had been shocked by a cattle prod. Family Affair's jockey snuck a peek behind him. His eyes were not visible behind his goggles, but I was sure they had become the size of medium eggs after seeing MayBell scoot into third and begin passing the second-place horse.

Family Affair's jockey brandished his whip and attempted to coax more speed from his ride. MayBell was now alone in second and quickly closing on Family Affair. They were neck and neck at the seventh furlong. Every spectator was now on their feet and cheering wildly, most of them for Family Affair.

The two thoroughbreds approached the finish line, still neck and neck. Family Affair's jockey continued to furiously crack his whip. But it was all for naught. MayBell nipped the favorite by a nose at the wire and won the race.

This heart-stopping result was not met with widespread approval. The loss of a sure thing seldom is. But in horse racing, as in life, there are no sure things, only favorites and long shots. And I'll give you some valuable advice about long shots. Never bet on one unless you're lucky or you know what you're doing. I may not always know what I'm doing, but I'm always lucky, lucky enough to have the right information at the right time. I suppose that's why San Francisco's upper crust frequently employs me to get them out of trouble. There are worse occupations.

I stored my binoculars, adjusted my tie, and went off to find my chauffeur, James. Do you know how hard it is to find a chauffeur named James? No, you probably don't. Well, let me tell you: it's damn difficult. It took me quite a while to find mine, so I wasn't too keen on losing him. "A proper chauffeur is worth his weight in spare parts," someone once told me. My James was certainly a proper chauffeur, always wearing leather gloves and never driving with one arm on the windowsill. Very fastidious.

I had successfully kept an eye on him all day until the final furlong of the final race. The favorite's dramatic failure had diverted my attention just long enough to allow him to vanish into the mob. I waded through the drunks and discarded programs and finally spotted him collecting a tidy sum at the payoff window. I have to admit that I don't him gambling. It's not that I have anything against a good wager; it's just that he was so hard to find. Do you know how hard? No, of course not. Anyway, the point is I don't want him to accumulate huge gambling debts and then run off to avoid paying them. He never seems to lose, though.

I was on my way to collect him and my winnings when I was intercepted by Bernie Ives, a highbrow sort of fellow with a home in San Francisco's pricey Nob Hill neighborhood, another one in Carmel, and I've been told he also owns one in Palm Springs. His face looked like putty and carried a perpetual look of mild disappointment. His eyes darted like moths around a streetlight, and they never focused on any one thing in particular. The wind tugged at his hair, but not a strand would budge because it was held tightly in place by a beeswax type of substance. His dark blue suit was made of fabric much too heavy for the weather, and that's a crime in my book.

I wasn't the only one to notice his fashion faux pas. A couple of polyester mugs also had their eyes on him. Now, if you ask me, wearers of synthetic fabric garments have no right to pass sartorial judgment on anyone. But there they were staring at Bernie as if he was a criminal.

"Winnie! What a surprise meeting you here," he said.

"Bernie, it's good to see you again. And my name's Winston." I hate Winnie.

"What a coincidence running into you," he said.

Nothing in Bernie's life was ever a coincidence.

"I haven't seen you in a while," I said.

"I just returned from Mexico. Thought I'd come here and watch the races." His feet shuffled like a stallion in a stall. I kept one eye on him, the other on James.

"What about you?" he asked.

"Me? I came here to place a few wagers, of course."

He nodded and looked past me.

"Say, I'm having a party tonight," he said. "Why don't you come?"

In case you don't know, Nob Hill parties are not to be missed. A summons to the pantheon of San Francisco's self-appointed gods is indeed a remarkable event; however, it is one that is expected to be observed with quiet smugness. Satisfaction with one's inclusion is best radiated, not shouted.

"Yes, I suppose I can do that," I yawned.

"Good." His face almost lost its look of disappointment. "I'm so glad I ran into you." He gave me one of those Hollywood handshakes and shuffled off.

James hid his winnings and strolled my way. The abnormal bulge on the left side of his chest betrayed his good fortune.

"Successful day?" I asked.

"Sir?"

I winked at him and started for my car. And what a sight it was! The magnificent bodywork sparkled in the sun, and the flying lady soared on the elegant chrome grill. I slowed my walk to admire what, in my opinion, is the world's most beautiful automobile: a 1963 Rolls Royce Silver Cloud III. I couldn't resist that car. The first time I saw it, I knew I had to have it. It was a steal, really. Its previous owner ran a limousine business. When his business suddenly fell into severe financial difficulties, I got the car, and he got the insurance money. I'd say that was an equitable arrangement all around.

James opened the rear door, and I poured myself into the luscious, leather-upholstered back seat. The fine Connolly hides emitted an intoxicating aroma and breathing it was like sniffing a glass of excellent single malt Scotch. James shut the door, and it closed with a solid, reassuring thud. He slid behind the steering wheel and tilted his head slightly toward the back seat.

"Home, James," I said.

I love those words! In fact, it's the only reason I wanted a chauffeur named James. I could have done a lot worse, mind you. My James, in addition to having superb driving skills, can fly airplanes and knows how to handle himself in combat. He knows a thing or two about horses, too, I suspect.

We returned to San Francisco, and he eased the Rolls onto Seacliff Avenue, a mansion-laden street that served as home to The City's aristocracy. Oh, and we locals refer to San Francisco as "The City," so that's what I'll call it from now on, if you don't mind.

Out on the bay, thin lines of fog drifted under the Golden Gate Bridge like fingers stretching into too-tight gloves. I was staying, uninvited, in a very comfortable house owned by a couple who were vacationing in Europe. You may raise your eyebrows, but they should never have left the place vacant. These old architectural jewels, like Italian sports cars, require constant attention. And who better to give them that attention than me? The neighbors never bothered me. In this neighborhood, no one ever bothers someone with a Rolls Royce. There is, however, the ever-present danger of the owner's unexpected, premature return. It's worth the risk, in my opinion.

With the car securely in the garage, I sauntered into the kitchen, pulled a Bass Ale from the refrigerator, and sat down in front of the panoramic living room window. The chair was very much like my Rolls: leather-covered with a great aroma, and was comfortably stuffed. The Bass Ale, however, was too cold. I suppose not everything in this world is perfect.

I turned my thoughts to Bernie Ives while waiting for the Bass to warm. What can you say about a man who made his fortune from pet mortuaries? I mean, really! Apparently, there is an abundance of pet owners willing to pay top dollar to see their furry loved ones go out in style. It's hard to figure out some people.

The thing about Bernie, though, was his total lack of self-discipline. To put it bluntly, he was a sucker. Women played him like a roulette wheel, and their numbers always came up. That weakness cost him quite a bit of money. Do you recall when he was mixed up with the daughter of an influential San Francisco political figure? Perhaps not. Bernie thought she was after him, but she was really after his pet mortuary. She wrapped him around her finger the way butchers wrap butcher paper around meat. Once he was properly wrapped, she started using his mortuary for some very unpopular cult activities. The potential scandal would have destroyed her father's political career and ruined Bernie's business. In the end, I saved the day by employing a fictitious film crew at Bernie's expense to convince everyone that the mortuary had simply been used to film a movie.

This kind of quick thinking encourages Bernie to call on me when he has girl trouble. The party invitation was, no doubt, a summons to duty. So, what had he gotten himself into this time?

*   *   *

The bay was smothered in fog when James rolled the Rolls out of the garage. A strong breeze blew the fluffy gray stuff over the Presidio and the links at Lincoln Park. The sun was setting somewhere, and it was getting dark. James flipped on the headlights, and we were off to the exhilarating heights of Nob Hill.

In case you don't know, Nob Hill is all high-rent townhouses and haughty hotels. The Rolls always gathers attention driving past them. The lights in the magnificent homes glittered like candles on an altar.

James guided the Rolls onto California Street and stopped at 1001. He slid from behind the steering wheel and opened my door, and I carefully emerged from the Rolls. A brass railing rose from the center of the concrete steps, and it glistened even in the fog. I climbed five steps to the entrance of a somewhat ordinary but tasteful building. A Chinese man in a tuxedo greeted me at the door. His thin hair was matted to his head with a shiny varnish. We fondly referred to him as the Peking Penguin because he always wore a tuxedo, and although he had been born in San Francisco and had never been anywhere near Peking (I know, it's called something else now, but I don't remember what). He was a real good man, someone you could depend on.

"Good evening, Mr. Churchill," he said with his usual tight smile.

"Good evening. Has Bernie remembered to put my name on the guestlist?"

"It's all right if he hasn't. You're always welcome here, Mr. Churchill."

"Thanks." Fine man, the Penguin. I pulled a few Cubans from my vest pocket and gave them to him.

"Oh, thanks, Mr. Churchill. You're a real good man."

"Smoke them in good health," I said. I turned away and

walked to the elevator, my footsteps absorbed by a red oriental rug that clung to an aged but highly polished marble floor. The elevator was already on the ground floor; I didn't have to wait for it.

"Have a nice time, Mr. Churchill," the Penguin said.

"Thanks."

"Hey, wait a minute!" he yelled.

I held the door open and peered into the lobby. A petite blonde stood before him.

"Another guest, Mr. Churchill. You wouldn't want her to have to wait for the elevator to come back down, would you?"

"Of course not." A true gentleman would never allow a woman to wait. I smiled and waited for her to enter.

"Thank you," she said in a voice as dry as the Sahara.

Elevators tell a lot about people. Most try to find something to read until they reach their floor. An elevator safety certificate must be the most widely read piece of paper in the world. Others try to make idle conversation. I prefer the readers. This woman was neither. She stared at me the way a viper stares at its prey. If she wasn't the cause of Bernie's troubles, she ought to have been. Her hair was a bit too blonde, her eyes a bit too deep, and her gait a bit too thoroughbred.

"Friend of Bernie Ives?" I asked.

She didn't answer. She just smiled a devious smile and then let her eyes roam over my tuxedo.

"I don't see many men dressing that way for parties anymore," she said. "You must be special."

"I do my best to uphold the highest gentlemanly and sartorial standards."

"You talk funny, too." She silently chuckled. "But I like it."

I nodded.

"Were you born this way, or did you have to work at it?" she asked.

"A bit of both, I suppose."

"No, you were born with it." She smiled again, a bit less deviously this time. "I can tell. I know men."

I smiled back, wondering what else she knew. The elevator stopped, and the door opened, and I put my arm across the retracted door and allowed her to exit first.

"Thank you," she said. "And yes, I am a friend of Bernie's. I hope before the night is over, I can be a friend of yours, too." She flashed her devious grin and disappeared into Bernie's party.

I embarked on a search for a glass of bubbly and waited for Bernie to find me. It didn't take long.

"Winnie!" Bernie's voice roared across his living room like a 747 at takeoff. And it was a big living room.

He still had beeswax in his hair, and he wore the same suit he had worn to the races. Quite inappropriate sartorial behavior if you ask me. Bernie was one of the growing numbers of people who no longer dress for the occasion. What a pity. It has nothing to do with money, by the way. It's all about style. If you have it, well, you know the rest.

Bernie slid past his quests and tramped across the room with the petite blonde firmly glued to his side. Her face puckered into a cynical grin at the mention of my name.

"Winnie, so glad you could make it," he said with more relief than joy.

"My name's Winston," I said.

"Winston?" the blonde chuckled. "Winston Churchill?"

"No relation," I muttered.

"Oh, this is Jill," Bernie nodded toward his companion.

"We met in the elevator," I said.

"Yes, he was a perfect gentleman." A sarcastic grin marred her pretty face.

Bernie smiled even though he didn't feel like smiling.

"I need to talk to you," he said. He glanced at Jill.

"I can take a hint," she growled. Actually, it was more like an angry purr. She tossed her head back and sulked off to wherever it is that women sulk off to when they sulk.

"Come on, let's go over here." Bernie led me to a small balcony overlooking the Mark Hopkins hotel.

"In some trouble?" I asked.

"Why would you think that?"

"You unexpectedly show up and the racetrack and invite me to your party. You only do that when you're in trouble."

"I always invite you to my parties." He was genuinely hurt, or as genuinely hurt as Bernie could be.

"And when I arrive at your party, you immediately need to talk to me."

"Just glad to see you. I want to catch up on old times."

"It's Jill, isn't it?"

"She's beautiful, isn't she?" His eyes brightened with his spirits.

I shrugged. She wasn't ugly.

"I suppose you're wondering what she's doing with a guy like me."

"Only those who do not know you well would wonder that, Bernie."

"Really?"

"Really," I said. "Now, what kind of trouble has she gotten you into?"

The brightness faded from his eyes like spent neon fading from a dying light fixture. "It's nothing," he insisted.

I didn't buy it, and he knew it.

"I just have something of hers that I need to return," he said after a pause. "That's all."

"Why haven't you returned it?"

He shrugged.

"What is it?"

"Nothing much."

"I see." But I didn't.

"I was wondering if you could return it for me."

"Let me get this right. It's nothing much, but you want me to return it to her instead of returning it yourself. Is it radioactive?"

"What?"

"Never mind. Why can't you return it yourself?"

"I think you'd be better at it."

"Bernie, I'm not in the delivery business." I turned to leave, but he stopped me by desperately grabbing my sleeve.

"Don't leave."

I looked at him the way a headmaster looks at a problem student.

"What aren't you telling me?"

Bernie looked out over the small balcony railing and into the street. He shuffled his feet before he spoke again.

"I couldn't believe my good fortune when I met Jill. I fell for her hard. Of course, I was worried she wouldn't stay with a guy like me. But I was so obsessed with her, with her beauty. I would have done just about anything to impress her."

"And you did." It was the typical scenario.

"And I did," he nodded.

"Tell me the worst."

He turned away from the street and faced me.

"Well, Jill is a real high roller. I didn't know it when I met her, but she has family ties."

"Nothing wrong with good breeding," I said.

"Family as in mafia," Bernie said.

"What?" Bernie had really done it this time.

"And that's the good part," he rolled his eyes. "You see, Jill knows I've got a plane, the one I use to spread a pet's ashes over the ocean."

"You use an airplane for that? Are you serious?"

"Yes. I cremate the pet, and after the funeral, I put its ashes into an urn and dump them over the ocean."

"Why don't you use a boat?"

"I enjoy flying," he shrugged.

"Oh." I guess I'll never understand some things. "So, what about Jill?"

"Well, she asked me to fly to Mexico, meet this man, and bring back some cocaine."

"Bring back some **what**?" I'll admit I was taken aback. If you know me, you know it takes quite a bit to throw me off my game. But if you know me, you also know I recover quickly.

"I wanted to impress her."

"Bernie..."

"So, I did it."

"How in the world did you get away with it?"

"I don't know," he shrugged. "You probably don't know it, but there's a legitimate organization that arranges group flying trips to Mexico. I was part of the group. The man I met in Mexico said it would be all right, and it was."

"So, where does the bad part come in?"

"Well, when I returned, I learned that the Feds are on to us, and they're just waiting for me to deliver the cocaine. If I deliver it to her, I'll be arrested, too."

"So that's how you got away with it," I said.

"What do you mean?" he asked.

"The Feds let you get away with it. It's a setup, Bernie. And you wanted me to deliver the cocaine to Jill. Bernie..."

"I never thought of it that way," he mumbled. "What should I do?"

"Don't deliver the cocaine."

"But if I don't deliver it to her by tomorrow, her mob friends will kill me."

"Doesn't Jill know the Feds are on to her?"

"I've told her, but she doesn't believe me. She thinks I'm stalling and trying to sell the cocaine myself."

"What kind of mob girl doesn't know when the Feds are on

to her?"

He shrugged and then turned his stare back to the street. San Francisco's summer fog had chilled the sidewalks, and the natives who walked below walked in heavy coats; the tourists shivered like oysters on a bed of ice. Several minutes passed before he spoke again.

"So, what should I do?" he pleaded.

"Where's the cocaine?"

"It's hidden in my mortuary," Bernie shivered. Poor lad.

"It must be well hidden," I said.

"Why?"

"I'm sure she's had the place searched."

"You think so?"

"Bernie..." I gave him a good Walter Matthau look.

"I suppose you're right. I hid it in a cremation urn."

"Bernie, that's rather brilliant!" I couldn't contain my surprise.

"Really?"

"Yes. I didn't know you had it in you."

He ran his hands over his beeswax until a guest spotted him and started toward us. The guest made a gesture toward him that was intended to be a wave but looked more like the hand movements of a pantomime.

"Will you help me?" he finally asked.

"I'll see what I can do."

Our conversation was cut off by the arrival of an aging femme fatale dressed in a metallic gown that looked as if it had been assembled from spare airplane parts.

"Bernie, how are you?" she asked, her intrusion made more irritating by a squeaky voice that sounded the way her clothes looked.

"I'm fine," Bernie said to her. Then he glanced at me. "This is my friend, Winnie."

I cringed. If he expects me to keep helping him, he's going to have to get my name right.

"Nice to meet you," she said in a strained monotone. She then ignored me and turned to Bernie.

"Guess what?" she said. "I received a call today from the Chestermans. They're in Belgium, and they don't like it. Can you believe that? A call all the way from Belgium. I've never had a call from Belgium before. Anyway, they've decided to come home early. I'm having my man pick them up at the airport tomorrow."

I was jolted by the news. The Chestermans owned the house I was staying in.

"I've got to go, Bernie. I've got to pack."

He looked at me funny.

"And my name is Winston!"

*　　*　　*

Okay, so this time Bernie had gotten himself into deeper trouble than usual. But I figured it would be fairly easy to get him out of it. I figured that Jill, although she roared like a lion, was just a pussycat. She didn't seem like much of a mob girl to me, and it was even possible that she was bluffing about that. I figured all I had to do was exercise my powers of persuasion and convince her that the Feds were on to her and the entire incident would be over. Clean and simple. I figured wrong.

*   *   *

Jill was a high roller, all right, the kind of woman you see attached to the arm of a prominent politician or clinging to the coat of a compulsive gambler on a Las Vegas winning streak. You don't find women like that at the Laundromat or in the check-out line at the local supermarket. You find them at places like the Starlight Room at the top of the Sir Francis Drake Hotel.

And that is where I found her, holding court with a small cadre of gadflies whose only goal in life was to be seen in the company of the right people at the right time in the right place. She wore a slinky, sparkling silver smock cut low at both ends, a very dramatic effect spoiled somewhat by a hairstyle more suitable to a dance club than a nightclub. The dress shimmered when she moved and when she moved, she moved in all the right places.

"Hello," I said.

She turned and stared at me the way she had stared at me in the elevator.

"Remember me?" I asked.

"Of course, I remember you," she replied. Her voice had not left the desert. "You're Bernie's friend, the one with the funny name."

"I see nothing humorous about Winston," I mumbled.

"Oh, yes, that's it, Winston Churchill," she laughed. "You're Winston Churchill."

One of her companions turned and faced me with a semi-sneer.

"And I'm the Duke of Earl," he driveled. Alcohol had severely impaired his motor skills. "But I'm a friendly Duke." He held out an unsteady hand, and the shift in balance nearly tossed him from his stool. "Nice to meet you."

Jill shoved him aside with a deep freeze shoulder and gave me her undivided attention.

"Well now, is this a chance meeting, or were you looking for me?" she asked. Her moist lips made it obvious which answer she preferred.

"Actually, I was looking for you."

"Now that's exactly what I wanted to hear," she purred. Her eyes blinked slowly.

"Hey," the drunkard on the stool slobbered. "Are you trying

to steal my girl?" The act of speaking was enough to once again disrupt his equilibrium. He steadied himself against the bar, and Jill's gaze pinned him there. "Okay, I guess you can borrow her." Another drink pushed him deeper into his stupor, and a tiny Martini river trickled down his cheek onto his shirt. "I'm a good duke..."

"Come on, let's go where we can talk," she said. She took my arm and led me to a table by a window. Outside, the City was once again being eaten by fog. Inside, I was determined not to be eaten by Jill.

"Now, Winston Churchill," she said in that way she had of saying my name as if it was a punch line. "Why were you looking for me?"

"Bernie told me about your little secret."

Her reaction made me wonder how many other secrets she had.

"Little secret? Just what do you mean?"

"I mean his little excursion into Mexico and the gift he brought back for you."

She was startled for just a second, and the startled look did not suit her.

"Bernie's got a big mouth," she said. "If he's not careful, someday someone's going to close it permanently."

I snickered to myself. She was a tough-talking temptress, just the kind of woman Bernie always fell for.

"So why did he tell you, and why are you telling me he told you?" she said. "No, let me guess. You're going to reason with me and explain why I should let Bernie off the hook. You're going to explain how much trouble we're in, and you're going to tell me it's for my own good." She raised her forearm to her forehead and attempted a Greta Garbo pose. Then she laughed a cheeky laugh. Okay, so it was not the response I had expected. Still, it takes more than that to throw me off my game.

"You do know the Feds are on to you, don't you? You're being set up."

"Ha! See, I told you what you were going to say. Bernie's told me that joke before, and it's no funnier coming from you." She threw in another cheeky laugh.

"What if it's not a joke?"

"Tell me, how could someone like Bernie know what the Feds are up to? He's way too innocent. And ignorant. Poor little man."

I have to admit that for a moment, she made sense, but there was no other explanation for Bernie's uneventful return from Mexico.

"But I had my people check it out anyway," she said. "And it's not true."

"Maybe your people are setting you up."

"Ha!" She hurled another scoff at me. "Another comedian."

"I am very disappointed in you," I sighed.

"Disappointed?" Her blush was genuine. "What do you mean?" She would have lit a cigarette if her diamond and silver cigarette case hadn't been empty. I wasn't going to fill it for her. Even a gentleman must draw the line somewhere.

"If Bernie was going to get himself mixed up with a mob girl, at least he could have gotten mixed up with one who knew the score."

She looked at me with that unique way that mob-girls-in-the-making look at men they don't like.

"I was beginning to like you," she said. "Now you're just boring me." She rose from her chair.

"I'd double check on the Feds if I were you," I said

"I'd mind my own business if I were you, Winston Churchill. I'm not impressed by your fancy clothes and eloquent talk. Because to me, that's all it is. Simply talk." She slithered back toward the bar, stopping once to flash me a final look of disdain. "And be careful," she purred. "Bernie will be in serious if he doesn't deliver, and so could you." She winked and returned to humoring the Duke of Earl.

This was not going to be as easy as I figured.

*   *   *

I spent my last evening in the Seacliff Avenue mansion sitting in front of a roaring fire thinking of ways to get Bernie out of his delicate situation. A plan didn't come easily, but when it came, it came to me as quickly as an ember snapping off a burning log. I immediately called Bernie.

"Winnie, have you found a way out for me?"

"Yes," I said. "You're going to deliver the cocaine to Jill."

"What! But you told me not to."

"I've changed my mind."

"What about the Feds?" Bernie gasped.

"Don't worry about the Feds. I'll take care of them."

"You will? How?"

"Don't worry about it. Can you arrange to cremate a dog tomorrow?"

"Yes."

"Good. Tell Jill you'll deliver the cocaine to her tomorrow and have her meet you at your plane at eleven o'clock in the morning."

"Okay."

"And my name's Winston!"

*   *   *

The fog broke early the next morning. It was one of those days where nothing could possibly go wrong.

"James," I said. "This is one of those days where nothing can

26

possibly go wrong."

"Yes, sir." His voice was a bit hollow, but that's how he is sometimes.

"Bernie told Jill to be at the airport at eleven. If you arrive by ten, we should be fine."

"Are you sure you will not need my assistance at the mortuary?" James asked.

"Positive. You go along to the airport. I can take care of things with Bernie."

"As you wish, sir." Sometimes that hollowness of his can be a bit annoying. But with the fog burning off and a toasty morning sun baking The City, nothing could dim my spirits. There's nothing quite like the thrill of the hunt to get the old juices flowing.

I finished packing and helped James load the Rolls.

"To the mortuary, James." Those words had no charm at all. Despite the absence of charm, he did a masterful job of easing the Rolls into the traffic.

Bernie's pet mortuary was in a very foggy neighborhood of small homes and ordinary shops. Even here, the fog was burning off.

James stopped the Rolls a block away from Bernie's.

"Good luck, sir."

"Thank you, James."

He left for the airport, and I walked to Bernie's pet mortuary. It was a white, church-like structure with a chapel in front and a workroom in the back. Bernie emerged from his workroom with a cremation urn.

"All set?" I asked.

Bernie nodded. His eyes were moist, and his face was long.

"What's wrong?"

"I always get emotional at times like this. It was a good little mutt, and I knew him personally. It makes me sad."

"If it's any consolation, that fine little mutt will save your fine little butt."

"I know, but it still makes me sad."

"What was its name?"

"Fifi."

"Fifi?"

"Yes."

I followed him to the small chapel. A genuine minister waited behind the altar, and Fifi's owners sat in the front pew. The wife wore a flowing, flowery dress totally inappropriate for a funeral, even if it was for a pet. The husband wore a suit that, from its poor fit, had been purchased at a time of slimmer anatomical proportions. And near the door were the two polyester suits from the racetrack. That was odd.

The minister started the ceremony, and Latin incantations

echoed off the walls. When the echoes ceased, the ceremony ended. The minister tended to Fifi's owners while Bernie took the urn back to his work area. I followed him and locked the door behind us. I had an uneasy feeling. Something didn't feel right.

Suddenly, the door handle turned. Bernie looked at the door as if it was a python ready to pounce. When the door handle stopped turning, the pounding started. It was, no doubt, the polyester suits.

"Who's that?" Bernie asked.

"You don't want to know."

"Shouldn't we let them in?"

"Not if you want to remain alive."

"What?" His voice had more cracks than the Black Rock Desert.

"Get the cocaine," I said.

Bernie took another cremation urn from the top of a high shelf.

"Is that all there is?"

"Yes."

I shook my head.

"What kind of mob girl is this Jill?" I muttered. "I mean, really. Why take such a big risk for so little cocaine?"

Bernie shrugged.

"Come on, let's go," I said. I grabbed the cocaine urn while

Bernie held Fifi's urn. We started for the back door, and Bernie reached for the knob, but I had to stop him.

"Hold it," I said.

"What is it?"

I peeked through a window near the door and saw two human bulldogs, much too conspicuous in their attempt to be inconspicuous.

"Do you know those canines?" I asked.

"No. Who are they?"

"I don't know, but it could be trouble. They could be Jill's men."

Bernie shivered and then jumped when the polyester suits increased their effort to knock down the door. Bulldogs outside, polyester suits inside. Quite a fix, I'd say. So much for nothing going wrong. I wondered what James would do in such a situation. I had an idea.

"Where's your car?" I asked.

"In the alley, about a half a block away."

"Give me the keys."

"What for?"

I gave him my urn.

"Hang onto the urns, and when you see me drive up, run to the car."

A frightened look crossed his face. The poor boy didn't have the stomach for this kind of stuff. Maybe the next time, he'll choose his women more discreetly.

"What are you driving these days?" I asked.

"A Mercedes." The words barely left his lips.

"What color?"

"Green."

"One of those sick, pea-green ones?"

"Yes."

"I thought so." People who do not dress for the occasion cannot be expected to drive properly colored automobiles. "All right," I said. "Wait here. I won't be gone long."

I opened the door quickly. The sound jolted the bulldogs into action. I ran for the alley. They pursued me. Fortunately, they ran more like bulldogs than greyhounds, and I was able to get a lead on them. I took a quick glance behind. The men were out of breath but still giving it the old college try. The polyester suits had left the mortuary, and they watched the bulldogs from across the street. I reached the Mercedes, opened the door, jumped in, locked the door, and put the key in the ignition.

"It's a diesel!" I cried out loud. And an old one at that. I'd have to wait for the glow plug to warm before starting the engine! I adjusted the rearview mirror to watch the progress of my pursuers. The bulldogs had nearly reached the bumper. The Mercedes was finally ready. I started it, rammed the gearshift into reverse, and backed into one of the men. He screamed and held his thigh. His partner, showing no compassion for his injured colleague, kept after me. He gripped the locked passenger door and tried to pull it open. I hit the gas and left him struggling for balance.

I drove down the alley and then punched the brakes with my left foot. The Mercedes slid to a halt in front of the back of the mortuary. I unlocked the passenger door and waited for Bernie. He didn't come out. I honked the horn. The bulldogs limped toward the car. They were hobbled by bruised bones but were not yet ready to give up the chase. I honked the horn again. Finally, Bernie timidly came through the door.

"Come on!" I yelled.

He ran and nearly dropped the urns. I couldn't watch. I opened the passenger door for him, and he got in. I mashed the accelerator to the floor and left the bulldogs behind us. James would have been proud of me.

However, I didn't have long to gloat. A car in the rearview mirror was following us. It was the polyester suits. I kept a steady pace, but they kept on me. Fortunately, they were delayed by a red light and heavy traffic which allowed me to beat them to the airport by a good margin.

The airport was small and south of San Francisco on the west side of the peninsula. Jill tugged on the plane's door. James was in the pilot's seat and prevented her from entering the plane.

"Hey, that's Jill!" Bernie said. "She can't get into my plane. Say, who's that in my plane? Who's not letting her in?"

"That's James. He'll be flying today."

"What?" Bernie disapproved, but he had little room to complain, and he knew it.

Jill saw Bernie and ran to the car.

"There's a man in your plane, and he won't let me in!" she howled. Then she noticed me. "You!"

"Me," I smiled.

"What's going on here?" she screamed.

"Just relax and do as I say."

"Why should I do anything you say?" Then she noticed the urns.

"Is that my cocaine?" she asked.

"You'll find out later," I said.

"Winnie, don't be so tough," Bernie said. He was beginning to soften. Jill could turn him into melting ice cream with one look from her torrid eyes.

"Let's go," I said, opening the door. "And hurry! And for the last time, my name's Winston!"

"I'm not going anywhere!" Jill screamed. "Give me the cocaine!"

"Look," I pointed toward the car speeding toward us. "Those

are the Feds, and they're coming for you and Bernie. Now get in the plane."

Jill's eyes narrowed then widened until they became the size of silver dollars. Then she did as she was told.

I grabbed Bernie, and she followed us to the plane. It was a nice, four-seat Cessna 175 Skyhawk. James opened the door, and I climbed in and sat in the front next to him. Bernie and Jill squeezed into the back seats. I placed the urns on the floor between my feet.

James started the engine, received take-off clearance, and taxied the plane to the runway.

"Why are there two urns?" Jill asked.

"As you can see, the Feds really are on to you. If Bernie had simply handed over the cocaine, you both would have been arrested. I don't really care about you, but I'd rather keep Bernie out of jail."

"So why two urns?" Jill repeated.

"To decoy the Feds," I said. "We're going to have to pull a switcheroo to outsmart them."

"Do both urns contain the cocaine?" she asked.

"No, only this one." I pointed to the one next to my left foot.

"What's in the other one?"

"Fifi."

"Fifi?"

"Doggie ashes."

"Oh, God!" She shook her head and looked at Bernie with complete, utter disgust. She crossed her arms and stared out the window.

James took off before the Feds could interfere. We flew West and were soon over the mountains.

"When do I get the cocaine?" Jill asked. The girl did have a one-track mind.

"After we put Fifi to rest."

The plane crossed the coastline, and when we were out over the ocean, James put the plane into an extended circle.

"Is this all right, Bernie?" I asked.

"Yeah, fine," he replied. He wasn't enjoying himself. Poor Bernie. Jill had belittled him, and he was sulking.

I nodded to James. I pulled my window open, reached for an urn, and quickly tossed it out of the plane.

"Hey!" Jill screamed. "Was that the right one?"

"Of course, it was," I said.

She reached around me and grabbed the remaining urn, opened it, and stared at the powder. It wasn't quite white enough. She frowned until her face contained more furrows than a newly plowed cornfield. She wet her index finger, dipped it into the powder, and brought it to her lips. Her face turned crimson, and her eyes nearly exploded.

"You're dead, Bernie," she shouted. "You're all dead!"

"What?" Bernie gasped. His voice creaked like old, wooden stairs. Then he looked at me. "Winnie!"

I ignored him. He's just going to have to learn to get my name right.

Bernie moaned and buried his head in his hands. Jill fumed all the way back to the airport. James landed the plane, and when he brought it to a stop, she immediately opened the door and jumped out. She was still holding the urn.

Quicker than charging polo ponies, a half dozen men surrounded the plane.

"FBI!" one of them shouted.

"Oh, no!" Bernie stepped from the plane and fell to his knees. Jill scowled.

"What do you have there?" the FBI agent asked. He was a sardonic little man, pudgy at the waist and gray on the head.

Jill kept quiet. The FBI agent stepped forward and peered into the urn.

"Cocaine?" A smug grin formed around his mouth.

I stepped from the plane and stood next to Jill. The FBI agent dipped his fingers into Fifi and tasted the powder.

"Poor Fifi," I said.

The agent got a strange look on his face.

"Hey, this isn't cocaine," he said. "What is it?"

"It's Fifi," I said.

"Fifi? What the hell's Fifi?"

"A dog. My friend runs a pet mortuary," I nodded toward Bernie. "He cremated the dog this morning. We had planned to dump the little guy's ashes over the Pacific, but the wind wasn't right."

The agent turned pale. I don't think he was very happy at having put dog ashes into his mouth.

"Let's get out of here," he barked. He took his men and went home.

"I think you owe me a debt of gratitude," I said to Jill.

She stared at me, viciously at first, then with some small degree of admiration as she realized I had saved her from jail.

"Leave Bernie alone," I said. "He's not worth the effort."

She looked down at Bernie. He was indeed a pathetic sight.

"You're right; he isn't," she said. Then she gave me a luscious Veronica Lake look. "But what about you? Are you worth it?"

I grinned and shook my head.

"Yes, but I'm not a family man."

I lifted Bernie by his collar.

"Home, James."

3 THE ROGUE GOES INTO A COMA

Critics will tell you that abstract art is simply an exploration of space, form, and color, that it's a mirror into our soul and intellect meant to make us question our perceptions and beliefs. But I don't buy it, and I just can't shake the feeling that abstract art is simply a scam to separate the gullible from their cash.

*   *   *

"No, those are not artists," Mary Bain snapped. "They're construction workers building the new exhibit salon."

"Oh," I said. I honestly couldn't tell. The works on display at the San Francisco museum named the Collection of Modern Art, COMA for short, were barely distinguishable from the materials the workers were using to build the new exhibit room, I mean salon. Besides, have you ever seen modern artists, particularly sculptors, at work? Trust me, if you haven't, they look a lot like construction workers.

"Follow me," Mary said, still smarting from my uncultured mistake. These art types have a very sensitive nature. "I'll show you where the sculpture was before it was taken."

Her blond hair brushed across the shoulders of a flowing, red Versace dress. The dress swished as she walked, and it reminded me of the broad stroke of a wide paintbrush. However, the small blue and green paint stains on her thumb and index finger clashed with her deep red nail polish. Not very artistic if you ask me.

I was at the COMA to investigate the disappearance of an expensive piece of abstract sculpture. Yes, I know, the racetrack one day, an art museum the next. A true gentleman effortlessly and elegantly operates within diverse environments. That means one must also have a diverse wardrobe. And if you know me, you know my wardrobe has something for every occasion.

In my opinion, an occasion such as investigating stolen art demands impeccable attire. I was, therefore, impeccably attired in an exquisitely tailored gray flannel suit with a traditional English cut augmented by a perfectly starched white shirt and a blue tie bluer than the waters of Lake Tahoe on a sunny day. A dark green spotted pocket square completed my look.

I suppose you are wondering why I was wandering about in

the milieu of modern art. Me of all people. If you know me, you know I prefer traditional art. I was at the COMA at the request of my friend, Lars Stinquist. Lars was a great patron of the arts and president of COMA's board of directors. He believed the missing sculpture was a serious matter, and clearly, I was in no position to disagree.

The theft was a complete mystery. One day the piece was there; the next day, it was not. The museum's security system was adequate, and video cameras spied on all the doors, but the tapes revealed nothing. Either the robbery had been committed by outstanding professionals, or it had been an inside job.

"It was right there," Mary said, pointing at a gray, wooden platform about three inches high.

"I see," I said, though I saw nothing. "What did it look like?"

"Here's a photograph." She held an eight-by-ten up to my face. "This is what it looked like."

I gazed at the photo of an L-shaped hunk of concrete, wood, and metal cable.

"I hope you can solve this mystery before the public learns of its disappearance. We can't afford to have their confidence in us shaken. We're supported almost entirely by their donations, and any bad publicity would be disastrous."

"I understand." I began to turn away.

She sighed deeply before she spoke again.

"I don't want to tell you how to do your job, Mr. Churchill, but don't you think you'd better keep the photo?"

I stared at her the way a jockey stares at a meddling owner who offers too much advice.

"Yes, I suppose so," I said, although I didn't see what good it would do me.

She glared at me, stuffed the photo into my left pocket, and patted it for good measure. She was quite attractive when she glared. In fact, she was quite attractive when she didn't glare. Her age was indeterminant, with every line and wrinkle expertly covered with makeup, giving her face the dignity of a Dutch portrait. Pity about those paint stains on her fingers.

"Mr. Stinquist has great faith in you, Mr. Churchill," she said. "I hope his faith is not misplaced."

"I always do my best," I said.

"Let's hope your best is good enough." She turned to leave.

"Oh, by the way," I said to her. "Do you think it could have been stolen during the day?"

"I doubt it," she said. "The security cameras are on twenty-four hours a day, and they would have captured any daytime robbery."

"What about the construction crew? They're here during the day."

"What on earth would the construction crew want with a work

of art?" she asked. "They couldn't distinguish art from their building materials!" She shook her head. "No, Mr. Churchill, I doubt they took it."

"I'm not implying they did. But don't they come and go? Couldn't someone have slipped in and taken the piece while the workers were out?"

"No. The backdoor is always closed and locked. The temperature in the museum must be carefully controlled to protect some of our more delicate pieces. We make the workers bring in whatever they need at the start of the day so they won't have to go in and out. Besides, Fred and I are always here. We would have noticed if someone had come in and taken the sculpture. The piece is very heavy, and no one could have moved it without getting caught."

"Who's Fred?"

Mary looked at me the way an exterminator looks at a termite infestation.

"Fred Nilless. He's the museum's director," she said. "Didn't you know that?"

"No," I said.

"He's an important figure in the modern art world. Anyone who knows anything about modern art knows Fred Nilless. He was very successful in New York before joining us. We are very privileged to have him."

"I guess I'm not too up on the modern art world," I said.

"I gathered as much." She pulled another look from her inventory of looks and looked at me the way a landowner looks at a serf who unexpectedly appears at the manor door.

Fortunately, James appeared and rescued me. Mary stared at him, her eyes a churning mixture of attraction and repulsion.

"Any luck, sir?" he asked me.

"No, James. It's quite a mystery. Where have you been?"

"Looking around."

"Did you see anything?"

"Nothing worth seeing."

"I have work to do, Mr. Churchill," Mary said, giving James another glance. "If you need me, I'll be around." She slithered off to wherever it is these art types slither off to.

I pulled the photo from my pocket and handed it to James.

"Is this the missing piece?" he asked.

"Yes," I said. "It's off the wall if you ask me."

*   *   *

Fortunately, I was staying in a house devoid of modern art, which was not a coincidence. One day at the COMA was more than enough for me. I had managed to find my way into a temporarily vacant Presidio Heights home and was enjoying its antique splendor. By the way, Presidio Heights is one of those old San Francisco neighborhoods that oozes 1890s charm.

I settled into a comfortable chair in front of a cozy fire and sipped Bass Ale until it was time to dress for dinner. You know how I feel about dressing for the occasion, don't you?

Lars had invited me to dine with him at the Pacific Union Club, a stuffy club of stifling proportions patronized mostly by washed-up near movers and shakers. Such a venue called for the utmost in conservative attire. I eventually decided on a dark blue suit with widely spaced, pale gray stripes and a predominately silver-checked tie. Very sensible, very suave, very Savile Row.

"The Rolls is ready, sir," James said.

"Very good, James."

We settled into the Silver Cloud III.

"To the Pacific Union Club."

"Yes, sir."

He set a course for the top of Nob Hill and efficiently conveyed me to my dinner destination. He then went off to wherever it is he goes off to after he drops me off.

Lars had already arrived, and he rescued me from the stuffed doorman who, despite my impeccable attire, was unconvinced of my worthiness to enter.

"What do you think, Winston?" Lars asked after we had been seated. Perfectly sculpted silver hair adorned the top of his head like a flag on a mast pole. He wore a conservative Brooks Brothers blue suit that was as stuffy as the Club's atmosphere. A tasteful foulard print tie sat symmetrically between the starched straight collar of a brilliant white shirt.

"No ideas yet," I said. "But I wouldn't be surprised if it turns out to be an inside job."

"Lord, I hope not. That would be very bad. In fact, that would be the worst scenario. What makes you think it might be an inside job?"

"There's no sign of a break-in."

"What about professional thieves? Wouldn't they be extremely careful and leave no trace?"

"I don't think they'd be perfect, and this looks like a perfect robbery. Still, with all of the construction going on, I suppose it's possible someone slipped in during the day and stole the sculpture."

"Yes, perhaps someone disguised as a workman or delivery person," Lars said.

"Perhaps. Mary Bain doesn't believe so."

"Mary Bain knows a lot about art, but I wouldn't expect her to be much of a detective," Lars said. He brought his napkin to his mouth and looked at me with raised eyebrows.

"Tell me about this Fred Nilless chap," I said.

"He's the museum's director. He handles administrative

matters, arranges acquisitions, sets up special exhibits, that sort of thing."

"Has he been with the museum long?"

"Five years. That's nearly as long as the museum has been open."

"How are things financially?" I asked.

"Getting by. We have a tight budget, but Fred does a good job managing our money. You don't suspect him, do you?"

"I don't think we can afford to overlook anyone at this point," I said. "Perhaps you should report this robbery to the police."

"No, not yet, Winston. We've got to avoid the bad publicity if we can. I want to give you a chance to solve it first."

"I'll do my best," I said.

"I know you will. I appreciate your efforts."

"You're welcome." I lifted my glass of 1982 Chateau Pavie in a toast to doing my best. The things I do for art.

*   *   *

A perfect night's sleep was cut short by a call from Lars. Another piece of sculpture had vanished. I rushed through my morning routine, something I hate to rush through, and James then rushed me to the COMA.

"Mr. Churchill," Mary said as if I had something to do with

the latest theft. "I can't believe this." She was nearly crying, and Lars consoled her with a soft pat on her shoulder.

"Show me the scene of the crime," I said.

Mary led us to another empty gray platform not far from the one that had once displayed the other missing piece.

"It's terrible, simply terrible," she said. She shook her head and gestured toward the platforms. "How could this happen again?"

"Perhaps it's now time for the police," I suggested. "I'm not a real detective, you know."

"Police?" Mary looked faint. Have you ever noticed how the mere thought of the police sends some people into a tizzy? Maybe you have, and maybe you're one of them. Well, Mary Bain was one of them. I'm sure there's some clinical explanation for why perfectly innocent people have such a police phobia, but I've never heard it. Apparently, it's contagious because Lars also developed the symptoms.

"No," he said. "I told you, Winston, no police. We can't have that. Not until you've done all you can."

"What more can I do?" I asked.

"Investigate," Mary snapped. "Isn't that what a detective is supposed to do? Snoop around. Do something. I've heard you're a very resourceful man."

She was correct; I am a resourceful man. But there were no suspects, no clues, no fun. I wasn't too keen on getting further involved, but one look at Lars and his sad-eyed, old hound dog expression convinced me to continue. A true gentleman never lets a friend down.

"What did this piece look like?" I asked.

Mary handed me a photo.

"This is the same one you gave me yesterday," I said, handing it back to her.

"No, it is not," Mary growled. She shoved the photo back at me. "The two pieces evoke totally different emotions."

I looked at it again. It still looked like a heap of twisted wreckage to me.

"I see," I said, although I didn't. "Well, I guess I had better snoop around." I leaned toward James. "Off the wall, if you ask me," I whispered to him.

He nodded discreetly, and I followed him to the back door. The rear entrance was the most likely place through which the sculpture had been removed and was, therefore, the best place to start snooping around, although the idea of snooping struck me as a bit undignified. Yet another sacrifice for the sake of art.

We examined the door and the surrounding area. The construction workers were making good progress on the new salon. Except for painting, the walls were finished, and the lights were nearly installed.

"We'd better check the alley," I said to James.

He reached for the doorknob. It turned freely. He raised his eyebrows.

"This door is supposed to be locked," I said.

The door opened onto a small alley and a small parking lot. A large trash bin occupied one of the parking spaces. I looked at James.

"It may be worth a look," he said.

"Go to it."

He frowned in that way he has of frowning without letting on that he's frowning, climbed up onto the bin, and peered inside.

"Is it in there?" I asked.

"I do not think I could tell, sir. There is a large amount of trash in here."

"It was worth a look," I said.

James dismounted and wiped the dust from his uniform. I thought I should look for tire tracks or use a magnifying glass to search for incriminating threads, but it seemed rather silly to do so.

"There's nothing out here," I said. "Let's go back in."

We turned but were stopped by the growl of a snorting bull. A yellow Lamborghini Urraco stormed down the alley toward us. The car screeched to a halt, and a well-dressed man in an Italian bespoke suit quickly emerged. He wasn't smiling.

"Who are you?" he yelled. "And what are you doing here?"

"Who are you?" I asked back. "And what are **you** doing here?" Sometimes you've just got to take a stand with these self-important types.

He cocked his neck.

"All right, if that's the game you're going to play then I'm going to call the police," he said.

"Good. I've already suggested doing that," I countered.

"What?" His demeanor flashed between bewilderment and consternation. "Who are you?" he again demanded.

"Winston Churchill," I said.

"Churchill?"

"Yes."

"Oh, you're the man Lars asked to investigate the missing sculpture."

"Yes. And who are you?"

"Oh, I'm sorry. I'm Fred Nilless."

We shook hands. So, this was the famous Fred Nilless.

"Sorry about being so aggressive just now," he said. "But with these robberies, well, you know."

"I understand," I said.

"Do you have any clues?" he asked.

"No."

Fred shook his head.

"This is terrible. How could it have happened again?"

"I'm becoming more convinced that it was an inside job."

"No, that can't be," Nilless said.

"Why not?"

"Mary and I are the only insiders."

"And you didn't take the sculpture?"

"Of course not! I'm the director of this museum!"

"What about Mary Bain?" I asked.

"You can't suspect her. She is an outstanding judge of artistic talent and a fine artist herself. She's also my right-hand man, er, woman. Without her, there would be no museum."

"Maybe she could use some extra cash?"

"I told you, she is above suspicion!" Nilless turned red and charged toward me like one of *Señor* Romeros' finest Miuras. I eluded him with a perfectly executed *chicuelina*. James stepped between us just in case.

"All right, all right," I said. "I had to ask. I'm just doing my job."

Nilless calmed down and straightened his tie.

"Yes, well, I'm sorry," he said. "Shall we go inside?"

We followed him into the museum. Lars stopped pacing long enough to greet us.

"Hello, Fred," Lars said. "I'm glad you're here. Winston, did you find anything?"

"Only Fred," I said.

"I'm going to see Mary," Nilless said. His Allen-Edmunds clicked on the shiny floor as he walked away.

"This Nilless fellow," I said to Lars. "Are there any scandals or anything like that in his past?"

"Heavens no," Lars said. "He has perfect credentials."

We were momentarily distracted by the raised voices of a man and a woman.

"Fred and Mary don't always see eye-to-eye about certain works, but that's what makes them such a good team." Lars winked at me.

I nodded. The argument sounded more like a lover's quarrel than artistic disagreement, but what do I know? I had already revealed my ignorance of modern art.

"Tell me, do you pay Fred enough money to drive a Lamborghini?"

"No. Mr. Nilless has business interests outside the museum. He must subsidize his income because we certainly cannot afford to pay him what he's worth. His work here is more like a labor of love."

"Oh, I see."

"Well, I've got to go," Lars said. "I'll be at my office if you need to reach me. And let up on Fred. He didn't do it."

* * *

Several visitors arrived shortly after Lars departed. I followed the trail of the voices and found two Asian men talking to Fred.

"It's good to see you again," Fred said to them. He said something else, but I couldn't hear it over the noise being made by the construction crew.

"Yes, we like the Prixley very much," one of the men said.

"I'm glad you like it," Fred said. "Perhaps you would like to see some of our new works?"

The men nodded. Fred led them to a painting that looked like a burnt pizza. He started to explain it but stopped when he noticed me. He smiled, but he didn't seem very happy to see me.

"Please continue," I said.

The Asian men politely bowed and smiled.

"I was just finishing," Fred said.

"Enjoying the museum?" I asked the visitors.

"Yes, we always enjoy it," one of them said.

"Do you come here often?"

"Yes, we come here very often."

Fred was inexplicably perspiring. It certainly wasn't hot in the climate-controlled museum. But it soon would be.

"Let me introduce you," Fred said. "This is Mr. Chiu and Mr. Chou. They're from Hong Kong."

"Hong Kong?" I said.

They nodded in tandem and smiled.

"That's a long way to come to look at pictures," I said.

They looked puzzled and turned to Fred.

"Language barrier," he whispered to me. He then ushered them into another room.

I could tell I wasn't wanted, so I stayed behind. Then another man entered the museum. He was dressed as if he hated fashion, and his thinning gray hair was combed back in such a haphazard manner that it made him look like a Billy goat. A pair of dirty rimless glasses clung precariously to the tip of his puffy nose. He carefully studied each picture in the main room showing particular interest in one that was a tangled mass of turquoise. He removed his glasses and used them as a magnifying glass. I stood next to him, hoping to learn a bit more about abstract art.

"This is a fraud," he said.

"It is?" I looked more closely at the painting. "How can you tell?" I continued. I anticipated an in-depth treatise on forgery, but that was not what I received.

"Because I painted the original!"

"What?" Art can be dizzying at times, can't it? "Who are you?"

"I am Lucius Prixley." He pronounced his last name "pree-lee". "And I painted that picture. Well, the real one, not that phony." He pointed at the messy painting with his glasses.

"Is that so?"

"Yes, that's so," Prixley growled. "Where's Mr. Nilless? He must know what's happened to the original."

"Why would Mr. Nilless know that?" I asked.

"Because I donated it to him personally so he could display it here at the museum."

"Is that so?"

"Yes, that's so," Prixley snapped. He reminded me of a dog going after an annoying flea. He frowned, and when he frowned, his face looked like one of those masks used to denote tragic drama.

"Who are you?" he asked. "Do you work here?"

"I'm just helping out," I said. I looked closer at the painting. The unmistakable aroma of a scam filled the air. Stolen sculpture, forged paintings, foreign visitors - it all began to make sense.

"Say, how fast can you turn one of these out?" I asked Prixley.

"I don't know," he fidgeted. "Good art cannot be rushed."

"Could you finish one by tomorrow morning?"

"I don't know. Why, do you want to buy one?" he asked.

"I know somebody who does."

"How much will they pay?"

"A lot."

"In that case..."

I arranged to meet Prixley the following morning, shuffled him out the back door, and went for James.

"Any progress, sir?" he asked.

"Yes, James. I believe these thefts have something to do with forged paintings and those Hong Kong visitors."

"Sir?"

"I've got it all figured out," I said. I told him of my encounter with Lucius Prixley. "Now, I'm going to set a trap. Those Hong Kong visitors are not here to look at art; they're here to buy it. Nilless is selling them forgeries."

"But sir, the forgeries are hanging on the walls."

Okay, so I may have gotten a few of the details wrong, but I was still convinced Nilless was up to some hanky-panky.

*　　　*　　　*

The coastal fog had retreated back over the ocean by the time I called on Lucius Prixley. He stumbled down the stairs of a weathered shack and stared at my Rolls Royce. Even an abstract artist can appreciate a Silver Cloud III.

"Is that your new painting?" I asked.

"Yes. I stayed up all night painting it."

"Let me see," I said.

He held up the canvas.

"Very nice," I said. "In spite of the coffee stains."

"I don't drink coffee," he growled.

"Oh. Anyway, I want you to offer this painting to Fred Nilless. When he accepts it, leave."

"Will Mr. Nilless pay me?" Prixely asked.

"No, I'll pay you."

"When?"

"After you deliver the painting. I'll wait for you outside."

"Okay."

Prixley enjoyed his ride in the Rolls. He sat pompously in the back seat and looked out of the windows through the corners of his eyes. He was visibly disappointed when the ride ended.

"Here we are," I said.

"Already?" Prixley asked.

James parked the Rolls in an alley around the corner from the COMA. Prixley reluctantly climbed out and carried his painting into the museum. Several minutes later, he returned empty-handed.

"Did he accept it?" I asked.

"Of course. They think very highly of me there. Do I get paid now?"

"Very soon."

James restarted the Rolls and drove to another alley about a block away from the COMA. The Peking Penguin waited for us there.

"Hello, Mr. Churchill," he said.

"Hello," I said. "Glad you could make it. I appreciate your help."

"When you say something's important, Mr. Churchill, I believe you."

"You're a good man," I said.

James hid a small radio transmitter in the Penguin's tie clasp and gave me the receiver.

"What's that?" Prixley asked.

"Bait," I said.

"Bait?" He stared at the transmitter through his smudged glasses.

Lars arrived and parked his Lincoln Continental behind my Rolls.

"I'm glad you could make it on such short notice," I said to him.

"What's this all about, Winston?" he asked.

"The mystery of the lost sculpture will soon be solved," I said.

"Really?" Lars stared at me the way a lottery player stares at a winning ticket. Then he noticed Prixley. "Lucius Prixley, what are you doing here?"

"He's helping us out," I said. "Would you mind writing him a check for a few thousand dollars?"

Lars scribbled a check and gave it to Prixley. Prixley brought the check to within an inch of his glasses, grinned, and stuffed it into his jacket.

"And who is that man?" Lars asked, pointing at the Penguin.

"He's a good man. He's also helping us out." I nodded to the Penguin and he started for the COMA.

"Listen to this receiver," I said to Lars. I ushered him into the back seat of the Rolls. James took his station behind the wheel.

"I'm almost there," the Penguin said. His voice came through the receiver strong and clear.

"Winston, what's going on?" Lars asked. "Is this some kind of gag? I appreciate a good joke but I'm very busy today."

"Just listen," I said. "All will soon be revealed."

We heard the Penguin open the door and walk into the museum. His heels clicked on the floor. The clicking occasionally stopped, and when it did, I assumed he had stopped to look at a painting. I think I heard him gasp once or twice, but that could have been my imagination. Then we heard another set of footsteps.

"Those sound like Allen-Edmunds to me," I said.

"Who?" Lars asked.

"Hello," someone said over the receiver.

"That's not Allen Edmunds," Lars said. "That's Fred Nilless!"

"Hello," the Penguin answered.

"I don't think I've ever seen you in the museum before," Fred said.

"No, this is my first time. My friends told me about it. You know, perhaps, Mr. Chiu and Mr. Chou?"

"Why, yes!" Fred burbled like a five-year-old boy on Christmas morning. "Are you also a collector?"

"Yes." The Penguin was nervous.

"Are you here to add to your collection?"

"Yes. I am interested in purchasing a Prixley."

"You are? Well, you're in luck. We have just received his latest work this morning, and it will make an outstanding addition to your collection."

Lars turned to me. He didn't look well.

"Hey! He's selling my painting!" Prixley said.

"That's it," I said. "Tally ho, James!"

James immediately started the Rolls and drove briskly to the COMA. He brought the Silver Cloud to a quick but dignified stop in front of the museum. We poured out of the Rolls and into the COMA.

"What's going on here, Fred?" Lars demanded.

"Nice job," I said to the Penguin. I stuffed a few Cubans into his pocket and pulled the tiny transmitter from his tie clasp.

"We heard the entire conversation," I said to Fred.

"What conversion?" Fred asked.

"We heard your attempt to sell museum property," I said. "We're onto your scam."

We then heard noises from behind the office door. James silently went to it.

"Don't open that!" Fred said. "That's a private office!"

James opened the door and exposed Mary Bain putting the finishing touches on a copy of Prixley's latest painting.

"You're in on it, too?" Lars asked.

"What are you talking about?" she snarled.

I gave her credit for playing it cool in the face of such incriminating circumstances.

"That looks like an imitation Prixley to me," I said. The easel contained a nearly complete forgery of Prixley's latest work. Makes you wonder why it took so long to paint the Sistine Chapel.

"What?" she said.

"We know all about the forgeries," I said. "We caught Fred in the act."

Mary's eyes widened until they looked like golf balls, and then she drove them at Fred.

"I knew you'd be the one to do us in," she screamed. "I knew you'd crack."

"They tricked me!" he pleaded.

"An ass could trick you!" Mary yelled.

"Mary..." Poor Fred's feelings were hurt.

"I suppose you're responsible for this," Mary said to me. "I knew you were going to be trouble. You can't trust people who know nothing about art."

"You should never have stolen the sculpture," Lars said. "Otherwise, I wouldn't have asked for Winston's help. We would never have discovered your little side business."

"We didn't steal the sculpture," Fred said. "Unless Mary did it on her own."

"I wouldn't touch those pieces of trash. You're the one who acquired them for the museum. You never did have any taste."

Lars turned to me.

"Then what happened to the sculpture?" he asked.

"Someone else must have stolen them," I said.

"No, sir, the works were not stolen," James discreetly interrupted.

"What?" Lars said.

"I found them in the new salon," he said.

"You found them?" I asked. "What do you mean?"

"Follow me," James said.

We followed him to the new salon, where he directed us to the room's far corner.

"There they are," he said.

The missing pieces were neatly embedded into the wall. The construction workers had mistaken them for building materials!

Lars' mouth hung open, and he couldn't close it.

"What have they done to those priceless works of art?" Fred cried.

"Put them to good use, I'd say," I said. "It looks as if they weren't so off the wall after all. Home, James."

4 THE ROGUE'S GAMBIT

"Pull!"

The clay pigeon sailed across the sky like a Lockheed Constellation at takeoff. Ted Nance followed its trajectory with his 12-gauge shotgun and pulled the trigger when the target reached its apogee. His shot splattered the little black and orange disk into hundreds of pieces.

"Good shot!" his wife, Nancy, said.

Nancy loaded her gun and tested its balance before bringing it to her shoulder.

"Pull!" she yelled.

Another clay pigeon flew across the sky, and she tracked it with the barrel of her gun and fired. Her substantial body silently absorbed the shotgun's recoil. Nancy's figure may not have been perfect, but her shot was. The clay pigeon returned to earth in pieces.

"Good shot, Nance," Ted said.

She grinned, lowered her gun, and turned to me.

"Your turn, Winston."

I hadn't done shooting of any kind in quite a while, and not even my Barbour Pennine shooting jacket's padded shoulders would prevent morning soreness. But that was no cause for complaint. I was in the country under a sparkling sky, breathing invigoratingly crisp air. Saving Bernie from his "mob girl" and uncovering an art scam had proven to be quite tiring, and a day of shooting was doing me good.

"Pull!" I said.

James launched the target from a small shack to our right. The clay bird sailed across the sky in front of me. I followed its path with my barrel, leading it slightly, then squeezed the trigger. The shotgun kicked me in the shoulder like a backfiring Ford, but my shot hit the target dead center.

"Good shot, Winston," Ted said.

"Thank you."

"Have you been practicing?" Nancy asked.

"No."

"Come now, Winston," Ted said as he readied his gun. "James must have given you a few lessons."

"Nothing of the sort," I said. "It was a lucky shot."

"Lucky my...," Nancy said as she gave me that skeptical look that schoolteachers give schoolboys with poor excuses. James took six more clay pigeons from a straw-lined wooden box and reloaded the launcher.

"What do you think of these clay pigeons?" Ted asked. "I imported them from Mexico, and their balance is superb."

I reached for one.

"Careful!" Ted said.

I decided to keep my fingers off them and peered into the box instead. The pigeons looked good and were nicely molded with "Made in Mexico" stamped into the clay along the edge.

"Yes, very good birds," I said. True skeet shooters are as picky about their clay pigeons as fanatical golfers are about their golf balls.

"I'm importing five hundred boxes of them for the sporting clays tournament," he said.

Now I suppose I should explain a few things. First, sporting clays. Sporting clays is a game invented by the British, of course, that combines skeet shooting and hunting. But instead of hunting real game, clay pigeons are used. Contestants move from station to station along a woodland course like golfers moving from hole to hole. The clay pigeons are launched and made to duplicate the movement of various game birds such as pheasant, quail, and rabbit. One point is awarded for each target hit. It's not as easy as it sounds.

And now on to Ted Nance. Ted ran a small but successful import/export business in San Francisco, shipping mainly to and from Latin America. He also owned the beautiful piece of land we were shooting on: one hundred acres nestled against the mountains separating the Napa and Sonoma valleys. He was an avid sportsman and an adequate businessman. He wasn't perfect, but he was a good man.

"You will be a member of my sporting clays team, won't you?" he asked.

"Of course," I said. "Who else have you recruited?"

"Nance, of course, and a fellow named Richard Rigger. He's my new banker."

Nancy's face momentarily clouded over even though the sky was clear. That should have given me my first clue something was wrong, but when the game is afoot, even if it's made of clay, and the sun is glimmering through brisk clean air, I mean, well, one can be excused for enjoying the moment and letting one's guard down.

"Richard Rigger?" I said. "I don't know him."

"He's throwing a party Friday night, and you can meet him there. You are free Friday, aren't you?"

"Come on, Ted, it's your turn to shoot," Nancy growled.

"Pull!" Ted yelled.

Another clay pigeon crossed the sky. Ted raised his gun to his shoulder, aimed, shot, and intentionally hit the target just before it landed on the ground. He turned toward us with a giant grin on his face.

"See if you can top that shot, Nance."

"I think I've had enough shooting for today," she replied.

"Oh." His eyebrows appeared to melt and drip into his eyes.

"You can stay here and shoot for as long as you like," Nancy said. "I'm going back to the house. Coming, Winston?" It was more of a command than a question.

"Sure," I said.

"You don't mind if James stays with me, do you, Winston?" Ted asked. "I would like to get in a bit more practice. And maybe James can give me a few tips."

"I don't mind at all," I said.

"We'll have coffee waiting for you," Nancy said.

*   *   *

"Winston, something's wrong," Nancy said as we approached the house.

"What do you mean?"

"Ted hasn't been himself recently. Something's troubling him. A wife can always tell. I don't know for sure, but I think it has something to do with this Rigger fellow. My intuition tells me

68

he's trouble."

"What kind of trouble?"

"I don't know. I'm sorry I can't be more specific, but Ted definitely hasn't been himself since he started doing business with him."

I looked at Nancy.

"These days Ted's always very nervous," she continued. "And he seems shifty. We both know that's not him. This Rigger fellow must be behind it all. Now there's a shifty one for you. I don't trust him a bit."

"Ted must trust him. He's on the sporting clays team."

"There's something fishy about that, too," Nancy said. "I don't think it was all Ted's idea."

"You think Rigger muscled his way in?"

"I suggested James for the team," Nancy shrugged. "He's the logical choice. But no, Ted picked Rigger."

"Well, you know how businessmen like to stick together."

"There's more to it than that. I know there is."

"Would you like me to look into it?" I asked.

Nancy stopped and touched my arm. "Oh, would you, Winston?" she said. "It would make me feel so much better."

"Sure."

"Be discreet, though, would you? Don't let Ted know I suspect anything."

"You know me," I said. "I am always the epitome of discretion."

"And always the perfect gentleman," she smiled.

*   *   *

Ted and James returned after the sun had turned the sky purple. Ted led me into his living room. An entire wall of shelves displayed knick-knacks from around the world. I examined a few pieces while Ted pulled some cigars from a wooden box.

"I've got something for you," he said. "Cubans, of course."

"Of course." I stuffed them into my pocket.

"Don't see why you want them, though. You don't smoke."

"Gifts," I said, thinking of the Penguin.

Ted nodded.

"Oh, and wait until you see this." He went to a handsome walnut gun case, unlocked it, removed one of the shotguns, and carefully carried it to me.

"Nice," I said.

"It's an AAHE-grade Parker. I paid $38,000 for it."

I raised my eyebrows.

"Yes," Ted continued. "It was a real bargain. I've seen them go for as much as $45k."

It was a beautiful shotgun all right. Not too much engraving but meticulously crafted. It oozed precision.

"Oh, he's showing you that," Nancy growled as she carried four steaming mugs of coffee into the room. "Give me a gun I can take out in the wilds and shoot with. All that one is good for is sitting in the case."

"Don't you use it?" I asked.

"No, it's a work of art," Ted said. "No true collector or lover of shotguns would ever take one of these out into the wilds. The risk of scratching it or damaging it is way too great." He put the gun back into the case.

"It's a waste if you ask me," Nancy said. "Give me a gun I can shoot."

I smiled. Ted locked the gun case and we settled into rustic, leather sofas.

"Now, Ted," Nancy said. "Tell us what kind of trouble Rigger's gotten you into."

So much for discretion. So much for not letting Ted know of her suspicions.

"What?" Ted said as he fumbled for a Cuban.

"There's something fishy going on, Ted. And don't deny it. I can always tell. I've asked Winston to look into it."

Ted shot me a glance that I'm glad did not come from the AAHE-grade Parker.

"Fishy?" Ted asked. "What do you mean fishy?" He looked like a golden retriever who had failed to retrieve.

"Yes," Nancy said. "Fishy. Now tell us about it."

"There's nothing to tell," he said. He cut off the end of the cigar like he was chopping the head off a chicken then lit it. It took him three tries before it finally caught. He inhaled, filled his lungs with pungent smoke, then exhaled, clouding the air around us.

"Nonsense," Nancy scoffed. Her eyes shot at him like the barrels of a Purdey side-by-side.

"Oh, Nance," Ted grumbled. "It's a business matter, nothing important. And it has nothing to do with you."

Nancy continued to stare at him with her loaded eyes. Ted turned to me for support.

"Really, Winston, it's nothing," he said.

"Come on, Ted, tell us," Nancy growled. She was going to get her way; it was only a matter of time. Ted could stall and fight it, but the outcome was predetermined. He did the sensible thing and saved us all a nasty scene.

"All right, all right." He ground his cigar into the ashtray, extinguishing it slowly so Nancy would fume. He leaned over and rested his elbows on his thighs and cupped his chin in his hands.

"I'm kind of being blackmailed," he mumbled.

That was a showstopper! Nancy looked as if she had discovered a slug crawling out of her coffee. I, of course, remained cool. A true gentleman maintains a dignified demeanor at all times no matter how big the surprise, especially when wearing Barbour hunting apparel. Trust me, I know about these things.

"And you could hardly call it blackmail," Ted continued. "Sometimes Richard has me bring things in from South America. I get them into the country for him without paying duty or customs."

"That's risky," I said. "Why do you do it?"

"Well, as you know, not everything I ship is strictly legal. Nothing harmful, mind you. I want to go on record for that. I'm very careful about what I import and export. Cuban cigars, things like that."

Nancy nodded.

"I never send dangerous contraband out. No weapons, nothing like that."

"Come on, Ted, get on with it," Nancy said. She had collected herself and was now quite comfortable playing the role of the chief inquisitor.

"All right, Nance, all right. Richard knows about my illegal imports and he knows that I haven't paid taxes on the income from them. He could get me into a lot of trouble with the IRS if he wanted to."

"Is he threatening you?" I asked.

"Not exactly. But he has dropped a few hints."

"But wouldn't he be in as much trouble with the IRS as you?" I asked.

"Well, I suppose so. But I have a feeling he has a way out."

"People like him always have a way out," Nancy growled.

"How did you get involved with Rigger?" I asked.

"I needed a banker to finance my new ship, the *Azul Pacific*. My other bankers wouldn't touch it. They said I was already too leveraged. Conservative fools! Anyway, Richard specializes in Latin America, so he was a natural choice. I didn't have to explain my business to him or justify my plans."

"How did he find out about your illegal imports?" I asked.

"I offered him a Cuban cigar, of course." Ted shook his head.

"Of course. So, what are these things he makes you bring into the country?"

"Oh, nothing serious. Cheap clay pots, things like that. Really, it's nothing serious."

"Ha!" Nancy said. "I knew Rigger was trouble. Why did you include him in our sporting clays team?"

"He kind of invited himself," Ted shrugged. "I didn't know he was interested in shooting until he asked to join the team."

"You should have invited James," Nancy said.

As you will see, she was right.

*   *   *

After the coffee and inquisition, James and I retreated to the Rolls. He opened my door but slipped something into my hand before I entered. It was a small stone bird.

"It's Moche, sir," James said.

I studied the small piece of sculpture.

"It's from between the first and eighth-century A.D," he continued.

The bird was about six inches tall with turquoise eyes and roughly carved wings. It looked both fragile and indestructible at the same time.

"Is it South American?"

"Peruvian, to be exact," he elucidated.

"Is it authentic?"

"Very."

I studied the bird more closely.

"James, isn't it illegal to take antiquities out of Peru?"

"It is, sir."

"Then I wonder how this bird found its way to California?" I asked. "I'm sure it didn't fly here on its own."

"There are ways, sir. Sometimes they are smuggled from Peru to Bolivia, coated in clay, and stamped 'Made in Bolivia.' They are then shipped to North America or Europe as cheap Bolivian pottery. Upon arrival, the clay coating is removed and..."

"Voila', a genuine Peruvian antiquity ready for someone's

private collection. Very clever."

"Indeed, sir."

"Where did you get this one?"

"It was on Mr. Nance's bookshelf."

*   *   *

Daylight dissolved into the bay like dark ink. The Rolls silently cut through the Friday evening traffic, and James brought it to a dignified halt in front of Richard Rigger's house. It was a modest six-bedroom affair in Cow Hollow - a pretty ritzy place by anyone's standards. James parked the Rolls, opened my door, and followed me into Rigger's party.

Cow Hollow parties aren't much different from Nob Hill parties. Perhaps a bit more nouveau riche and therefore a bit more pretentious. The Claude Montana set instead of the Yves St. Laurent crowd. I had thrown caution to the wind and wore Italian: a nice solid gray Brioni suit with a striped shirt and striped tie. I know stripes on stripes aren't advisable, but the shirt and tie colors were complementary enough to make it a perfect look. Style, you either have it, or you don't, and if you have it, you have it all the time.

I followed James into Rigger's library. It was in a high-ceilinged room containing more people than books. We mingled with the guests, although I would have preferred the books.

"Careless storage," I said, pulling a cigar from a leather pencil holder conspicuously adorning a Louis-the-something antique desk. Take my advice, always store your cigars in a humidor. If you don't, your cigars won't burn properly, not taste good, and may even become infected with tobacco beetles! Elie Blue makes a nice humidor of Spanish cedar. I don't smoke, but I know this on good authority. But I digress."

I sniffed the cigar and gave it to James.

"Cuban," he said after sniffing it.

I nodded. I was about to place one in my vest pocket when Ted and Nancy found us and introduced us to our host and new shooting partner.

"Winston, I'd like you to meet Richard Rigger," he said.

Rigger was a barrel of a man with a cigar stuck in his face, and three strands of hair stretched across the top of his head. Not sporting material, if you ask me. Yes, looks can be deceiving, but, I mean, a man who wears a blazer and pants of contrasting shades of dark blue? Really! Nothing good can come of a man like that.

"Winston is the other member of our sporting clays team," Ted said to Rigger.

"Yes, I've heard of you," Rigger said. "Any friend of Ted's is a friend of mine."

"Thank you," I said.

"Yes, meeting Ted was a mutually fortuitous event," Rigger

continued.

"I understand you financed the purchase of Ted's newest ship," I said.

"Yes, that's how we met. We both have business interests south of the border, so it was a natural partnership." His flabby hand patted Ted on the shoulder.

"So, you have a banking business in Latin America?" I asked.

"Yes. I have clients there. Wealthy clients, of course. Clients who invest considerable amounts of money through me. I can offer them much better investment opportunities here than they can find at home. Those countries are so unenlightened when it comes to investing. I help my clients find more productive outlets for their assets."

"I see," I said.

"And they're always grateful for my services and reward me appropriately. That allows me to indulge in my hobbies."

"Like shooting?" I asked.

"Yes, like shooting." He closed one eye and aimed an imaginary gun at an imaginary target.

"Bang," he said. Then he laughed.

"He's no shooter," James whispered to me.

James was right. A real skeet shooter keeps both eyes open. If you don't believe me, ask Holland & Holland's shooting school outside London.

"Speaking of shooting, when are those clay pigeons arriving?" he asked Ted.

"Early Saturday morning," Ted said.

"The day of the tournament," Rigger said.

"Yes."

"That's cutting it close. I'd better pick them up."

"There's no need for that, Richard," Ted said. "Don't go out of your way. I'm sure it would be an inconvenience, and you'd have to get up very early."

"That's not a problem," Rigger said. "Those are exceptional clay pigeons, and I don't want to see anything happen to them."

"I see your point," Ted said. "But my men can handle it."

"Will you be there personally?" Rigger asked.

"No, but..."

"We can't take chances then, can we?" Rigger said.

"No, I suppose not," Ted agreed.

"I don't think the clay pigeons will fly away on their own," I joked.

Rigger stared at me in a way that almost made me believe they would.

"Those are valuable clay pigeons," he said sternly. "I don't want anything happening to them."

"Yes," Ted said, rising to Rigger's self-importance. "That would be very bad. The shooting club is counting on those birds."

"Then it's all settled," Rigger said. "I'll pick them up and deliver them to the club. They are arriving on the *Azul Pacific*, aren't they?"

"Yes," Ted said.

"Good. What time does the ship arrive?"

"Around four. Unloading begins at five-thirty."

"I'll be there with my men and truck," Rigger said.

"If you insist," Ted said.

"I insist," Rigger smiled. "It was nice meeting you, Winston," he said, shaking my hand. He then melted back into his party.

"He's awfully worried about those clay pigeons, isn't he?" I asked Ted.

"Yes," Ted said. "But they are good ones, aren't they?"

"Yes, they are. But they aren't gold, are they?"

He looked at me the way a French waiter looks at an American diner.

"Of course not," he said.

Nancy frowned at him.

"Oh, Ted, they're just a bunch of clay disks."

Ted ignored her.

"I'm ready to go home," Nancy said.

"So soon?" Ted replied.

"Yes."

"If you say so. I'll see you next Saturday at the tournament," Ted said.

*   *   *

The sporting clays tournament site resembled a small circus. Food, clothing, and gun vendors sold their wares under small khaki tents in a clearing next to the parking area. A large, white tent had been erected to accommodate the couple of hundred spectators who would stay for the post-tournament dinner. Have you ever noticed how there always seems to be more watchers than doers? No, you probably haven't. Well, I have, especially where sporting clays are concerned.

James parked the Rolls in a secure spot and began preparing my shooting gear. He opened the boot and removed my Wellingtons and Barbour shooting waistcoat - it was a bit too warm for a full jacket. Take my advice and never participate in a shooting event without the appropriate attire. There are practical reasons in addition to cutting a stylish appearance. My Barbour waistcoat was padded in all the right areas and provided unmatched protection from the elements. Ted had lent me a beautiful Baretta over-and-under shotgun for the event, and James was checking it over.

"I'll ready the gun, sir."

"Thank you, James."

"Winston!" Ted said, wearing a pair of sporting knickers that would have looked quite spiffy on a man thirty pounds lighter.

"Good morning, Ted."

"It may not be such a good morning," he said in one of those overly serious voices.

"What's wrong?"

"Richard just arrived. He was delayed by a traffic accident on his way to the ship, and when he finally arrived, the clay pigeons were missing!"

"Relax," I said.

"Relax? I promised the club I would supply the birds for this tournament! It can't go on without them!"

"They are already here," I said.

"What?"

"I took the liberty of having James pick them up. He was near the docks anyway, and I knew you wouldn't mind. He brought them straight to your shooting club. And lucky for us, he did, with Rigger having had that accident."

"Oh," Ted said. His eyebrows and spirits rose like the sun rising over New Mexico's Sandia Mountains.

"Sorry I forgot to tell you."

"That's okay. The clay pigeons are here, and that's all that matters!"

I smiled.

"Here comes Mr. Rigger, sir," James said.

One can always tell when a man is nervous, even if he's a hundred yards away. It has something to do with the lopsided way his head sits on his neck.

"Ted, have you found those clay pigeons yet?" His voice would have frightened even the most hardened alley cat.

"It's all right, Richard," Ted said. "Winston had his chauffeur pick them up. They're here, and there's nothing to worry about."

Do you recall what it's like when you flip on a light switch, and the 100-watt light bulb suddenly pops with a momentary flash of incandescent light before plunging the room back into darkness? If you do, you have some idea of the expression on Rigger's face. He swallowed with such deliberateness that I thought his entire face would be drawn down his gullet. It wasn't.

"I told you I would pick them up!" he screamed. His vocal cords stretched like rubber bands.

"Sorry, old sport," I said to him. "James was nearby."

"It's okay, Richard," Ted grinned. "The pigeons have been delivered. The tournament will go on!"

Ted patted Rigger on the back and nearly knocked him over.

*   *   *

Ted beamed as we waited for the tournament to begin. The officials had complimented him on the quality of the clay pigeons, and to him, that was almost as good as winning the event. However, Richard Rigger was not beaming. He appeared to be in the grip of something akin to opening-night jitters. Nance was unsympathetic. Her gaze was cold, but her emotions were steaming. I, of course, maintained my composure. I have already told you that when one owns a Rolls Royce, one's behavior must measure up. I have told you that before, haven't I?

The first shooting station duplicated the movement of rabbits and pheasants. The targets were launched in pairs, those simulating pheasants crossing high and fast, those simulating rabbits bounding along the ground so realistically that you could almost see furry tails. Rigger carefully watched each contestant's shot, following the flight of each clay pigeon as it sailed through the trees or along the grass. He watched where the pieces landed when they were hit and even where the un-hit targets touched down.

"You're awfully intent on the targets," I said to him.

"What? Oh, I'm studying the trajectories."

I figured Rigger would use his newly acquired knowledge of trajectories to improve his shooting. I figured wrong.

Ted was the first to shoot for our team, and he hit just two of his ten targets.

"They're just like real pheasants," he grumbled.

Rigger shot next. The uncertain manner in which he held his

gun did not inspire confidence. And, as you probably guessed, he wasn't appropriately dressed. He looked more like a clam digger than a shooter. Somewhat an embarrassment, actually.

"Pull," he crackled.

Two clay pigeons sailed toward the trees. He watched the first one intently but forgot to shoot at it. The second was nearly out of range before he finally pulled the trigger. That was followed quickly by a clay pigeon that bounded along the ground. He also forgot to shoot at that one. When the smoke had cleared, he had missed all ten shots. So much for studying trajectories.

"Bad luck," Ted said to him, bestowing a conciliatory pat on the back.

"Bad shooting," Nancy muttered to me.

Nancy salvaged the round for us by hitting five of her shots, and I'll admit that my four-for-ten didn't hurt either. We left the first station a bit rattled but still resolved to giving it the old college try. Rigger looked back as if he was trying to figure out what had gone wrong.

The second station was in front of a glistening pond. The clay pigeons were launched at the waterline level to accurately simulate mallard ducks. It was very authentic and promised to be one of the more challenging stations.

Again, Rigger watched each bird as it was launched. I was sure it would be only a matter of time before he figured it out, and when it was his turn to shoot, he did show improvement. He remembered to shoot at the first clay pigeon. He didn't hit it, but he did shoot at it. He did, in fact, shoot at all of them. He didn't hit any of them, but at least he shot at them.

"You need to relax, Richard," Ted said to him.

"He needs to learn how to shoot," Nancy whispered to me.

"Ted's right," I said to Rigger. "You're too concerned about trajectories and all that."

"Just aim and shoot," Nancy growled.

The third station simulated springing teal. The clay pigeons were launched across another pond. Unfortunately, by this time, Rigger was utterly demoralized.

"He's a bundle of nerves," Nancy whispered.

"He certainly seems distracted," I said.

"He's going to cost us the tournament," she added.

"Relax, Nance," Ted said to her. "It's still early."

We pointed Rigger toward the next shooting station, gave him a helpful little push, and watched him ready his gun.

"Pull," he said so softly that the launcher did not hear him. "Pull," he repeated.

A clay pigeon flew across the sky, then another quickly behind it. Rigger fired two shots into the air and watched the un-hit disks hit the water. One of them skipped several times before submerging.

And that's how it went. He hit only one of a hundred attempts, and it appeared to me that he had hit that one by accident. A bit of a burden on the team he was.

"I told you you should have invited James," Nancy growled at Ted.

He ignored her and turned to Rigger.

"Are you feeling okay, Richard?" he asked. "You don't look well."

"Yes, cheer up, old man," I said. "After all, we didn't lose a fortune, only the shooting tournament."

He looked at me strangely.

"Fortune?" he said. "What do you know about fortunes?" He turned and left in a huff.

"Well, I never," Nancy said. "His poor shooting costs us the tournament; then he acts like some prima donna."

"He's had a bad day," Ted said.

"You don't know how bad," I added.

Nancy looked at me funny.

*   *   *

The organizers presented an excellent post-tournament dinner. Real game birds, not clay ones, were served in a light butter sauce with plenty of Napa Valley's finest wine. Very tasty. All in all, a first-class meal. It was a shame Rigger didn't have an appetite. He picked at his meal with disinterest. Something was eating him. He finally pushed his plate away and left the table.

"Where's Richard going?" Ted asked. "I hope he doesn't wander too far away and miss the awards ceremony."

"Why?" Nancy asked. "Are they giving an award for the worst shooter?"

"Nance, that's not a nice thing to say," Ted said.

Nancy tossed her napkin onto the table and rose. Someone struck up the band and diners became dancers. We became separated in the ensuing mayhem. I eventually found Ted extricating himself from a human sandwich.

"Where's Nance?" Ted asked.

"I don't know," I said. "Someone said they saw her going back to the shooting course."

"Why would she go back to the course?" Ted asked.

"She is following Mr. Rigger, sir," James said, appearing next to Ted.

"What? Why is she doing that? And what's Richard doing?"

"He is looking for something," James said.

"What on earth for?" Ted asked.

"A pot of gold," I said.

Ted looked at me funny.

* * *

James knew a shortcut to the shooting course, and we intercepted Nancy near the dove shooting station.

"Nance, what are you doing here?" Ted whispered.

"Rigger's up to something," she said. "I aim to find out what it is."

"I think you're about to find out," I said.

James led us into a clearing where we found Rigger rummaging through the foliage and breaking apart undamaged clay pigeons. James' flashlight shed some light on the scene.

"Looking for something?" I said.

Rigger jumped like a startled quail.

"What?" he yelped. "Who are you?"

"It's me, Winston Churchill," I said.

"Churchill? Churchill! I should have known. It's all your fault, you know! I was supposed to pick up those clay pigeons, not you. But you had to interfere, didn't you? You ruined everything. Now they're gone, those precious, valuable, irreplaceable..."

"You mean the Peruvian antiquities?"

He stared at me, surprised at first, then confused, then angry.

"You mean you knew the antiquities were in the clay pigeons?" he screamed. "And you let them get shot to pieces? Oh, how could you? You're inhuman!" Rigger fell to his knees.

"Don't worry," I said. "I took the liberty of substituting ordinary clay pigeons for those containing antiquities. You didn't think I'd let those priceless artifacts get destroyed, did you?"

"What?" he looked up at me. "Then where are they?"

"On their way back to where they belong. And now you're going to where you belong."

"You can't send me to jail. I have friends in high places. You can't prove anything!"

"Jail? I'm not sending you to jail. I'm sending you to the Peace Corps."

"The Peace Corps?"

"Well, something like it," I said.

Two men silently emerged from the shadows and stood next to Rigger.

"It's time for you to repay your debt to society," I said. "These men will help you do that."

They lifted Rigger to his feet and led him away.

"*Adios*," James said.

"*Adios, amigo*," one of the men replied.

"Winston, what's going on?" Ted asked. The poor boy was a bit confused.

"The clay pigeons you imported from Mexico contained stolen Peruvian antiquities that Rigger was smuggling into the country. His Latin American clients molded some very old and very valuable gold and turquoise necklaces into the clay pigeons. They fit perfectly. Rigger planned to intercept the pigeons when they arrived on the *Azul Pacific* and substitute ordinary ones in their place. James, of course, beat him to it."

"So, throughout the tournament, Rigger thought we were shooting at the antiquities-laden clay pigeons," Nancy said.

"Correct."

"No wonder he shot so poorly," she said. "He thought a fortune was disintegrating with every shot. I told you he was trouble," she said to Ted, slapping his arm.

"Where are these Peruvian things now?" Ted asked.

"On the *Azul Pacific*," I said. "On their way home."

"That can't be," Ted said. "The *Azul Pacific* isn't leaving port until next week."

"Ah, yes," I said. "There's been a slight change in plans. Smuggling antiquities back into Peru is almost as difficult as smuggling them out. Naturally, the people I arranged to undertake this task require compensation, and the *Azul Pacific* is that compensation."

"What?" Ted asked. "You gave away my ship?" His face looked like a blank billboard.

"It's a small price to pay, don't you think, after all the trouble it nearly got you into."

"But..." Ted's voice faded, and Nancy's penetrating stare reminded him that he was in no position to argue. "How did you know about the antiquities?" he asked.

"A little bird told me," I said. "Home, James."

5 THE ROGUE TO THE RESCUE

In my opinion, the Silver Cloud III was the last of the true Rolls Royces. It was the last model built with a separate chassis allowing the finest coach makers such as Thrupp and Maberly to supply elegant, custom bodies. Silver Clouds, like the James Young Continental saloon and the Mulliner Park Ward coupe, have character. The new models, although full of hides and polished wood, lack character. They connote wealth but not necessarily good taste.

James floated my 1963 Silver Cloud III down Post Street and glided it to an imperceptible stop in front of the Kensington Park Hotel. It was a nicely appointed inn occupying what was once exclusively the Elks Building. I had been unable to secure a proper residence and was therefore staying in a hotel. Mind you; I could have done worse. The Kensington Park's inviting lobby with its warm Spanish wood ceiling was reassuring in an Old

World way. Tea and sherry were served daily in front of the lobby's tastefully designed fireplace. It was all very civilized.

James exited the Rolls and leered at the car double-parked in front of us. Yes, it was one of those tasteless new Rolls Royces with as much style as overcooked pasta. The owner of the new Rolls, a flamboyant man in a $3,000 red overcoat, emerged from the hotel, gave the doorman a $50 tip so all could see, did the same with the valet who had retrieved his car and recklessly slid behind the wheel. The tires chirped on the cool pavement as he sped off.

"Distasteful, isn't it, James?" I was referring to both the car and the clothes. When it comes to clothes, it's not how much you spend but how you wear them. Some people can break all the rules and still look devastatingly dapper. Others? Well, style, you either have it, or you don't, and if you have it you have it all the time.

James gave me a discreet nod. The valet offered to park my car, looking forward to another $50 tip, but James would have none of it. Good chauffeur, that James, worth the difficulty of finding.

I was returning to the Kensington Park Hotel to meet Caroline Avalon for tea. She was the daughter of Harry Avalon of Avalon Industries fame. I had known Harry for a long time and had done several "odd" jobs for him. I had run into him at the Post Street

Bar and Cafe earlier in the week.

"I'm a man of leisure now, Winston," he had said to me. "My daughter, Caroline, runs the business, and she's doing a damn fine job of it, too."

There was a pause as he attempted to relight his pipe. It wouldn't light, so he placed it on the table and looked at me the way firefighters look at smoldering ashes.

"Have you read the Wall Street Journal today?" he asked.

"No, I'm afraid I haven't. What have I missed?"

He took a copy from his lap and tossed it onto the table. It was folded to reveal a headline: "Halzbee Attempts Takeover of Avalon Industries." Harry sarcastically chuckled to himself.

"I take it you're not in favor of this takeover attempt?" I said.

"Don't be stupid, Winston! Of course, I'm not in favor of it. Halzbee's a vulture of the worst kind. Look at this."

He opened the Journal to a full-page ad placed by this Halzbee character. The ad was an impassioned plea to Avalon Industries shareholders to sell him their stock, and it contained no kind words for Avalon's current management team.

"What does this mean?" I asked.

"It means we -- I mean Caroline -- could lose the business."

"Really?"

"Yes, really. Listen, Winston. Avalon Industries is a good business. It's profitable, returns a good dividend, and is solid as a rock. I made it that way. We have no debt to speak of. We've been conservative, but by God, we're still here today, whereas most of our competitors are not." He poked the newspaper with his powerful index finger.

"Now, along comes this scavenger Halzbee, planning to borrow against Avalon Industries' assets to buy the company, and it's disgusting."

"Wait. Let me get this straight. He's going to borrow money to buy Caroline's company, using the assets of her company as collateral for the loan?"

"Yes. You can be sure he's got some fancy investment banker who will issue junk bonds to finance the takeover."

"Does that make sense?"

"Don't beat around the bush, Winston. You're asking if Avalon Industries is worth it. Well, here's the deal. If you sold all of the assets that make up Avalon Industries, you could probably get around $180 million for them. With approximately two million shares of outstanding stock, that works out to $90 a share."

"What is today's stock price?"

"Fifty-five."

"Oh." And there was the problem. "The company is worth more broken up than whole," I said.

Fireworks exploded in Harry's face while his skin turned the color of a fine Napa Valley merlot.

"Damn it, Winston!" His fist rattled the table. "A company is more than numbers on a piece of paper. It's a going concern that employs people, real people with real families. These people buy goods and services from other businesses. That's what makes our system work. It's all part of the greater plan. Not to mention that we -- I mean Caroline -- donate an awful lot of money to community projects. You see, Winston, it's not just about paper profits."

"You're right, of course." Harry had a talent for making you feel like you had been caught with your hands in the cookie jar. My agreement with his position only slightly calmed him.

"Do you think Halzbee can get away with it?" I asked.

"You're damn right he can! He already owns seven percent of Avalon Industries, making him one of our larger shareholders."

Harry reached for his pipe and tried once again to light it. Once again, it would not light.

"Listen, Winston, I should have kept a majority of the stock when I took the company public, but we needed all the cash we could get, so I kept only fifteen percent. I put the company's interests before mine, and now I'm -- I mean Caroline -- is paying the price."

"Come on, Harry. You know you did the right thing."

Harry grunted.

"I suppose I did. I'm just frustrated. Halzbee plans to offer $74 a share, and I can't stop him from doing it."

"That's a hefty premium over the current price."

"Avalon Industries shareholders are basically a satisfied group. His offer has to be very rich for them to sell. And his offer is very rich."

"How can he afford to pay that much?"

"It comes down to what it's costing him to finance the deal. His investment banker will charge him an arm and a leg in fees, and he'll have to subtract that from whatever profit he makes. The higher the fees, the less he can profitably afford to pay for the stock. We -- I mean Caroline -- can pay him off and repurchase the stock at a higher price than he paid for it. It's called paying greenmail. Or let him make the offer. If the shareholders go for it, and I think they will, he'll own the company and sell off the assets making a tidy profit at our expense."

"Yes, if the company is worth $90 a share broken up and he pays $74, he makes $16 a share."

"Not quite. As I said, you have to subtract the interest expense on the junk bonds and those fees he's going to be charged by his investment banker. Once you figure those in, he's probably paying about $86 a share."

"Still, on 2 million shares…"

"Yes, Winston, that's eight million dollars profit." Harry shook his head. "Small change by Wall Street standards but not a bad piece of change for a two-bit hustler like Halzbee."

"Unfortunately, it's not illegal, is it?"

Harry leaned forward and looked me straight in the eye.

"No, making a junk-bond financed offer is not illegal, but the way he acquired his seven percent share of Avalon Industries was," he said.

"What do you mean?"

"Listen, Winston. He used strong-arm tactics to get people to sell him their stock, and that's called extortion. And he'll probably use strong-arm tactics to acquire the rest of Avalon Industries."

"Can you prove that?" I asked.

"Well, no. But I know it's true."

"Still, without proof…"

"I know, I know. If I had proof, I wouldn't need your help."

"Ah, then this wasn't a chance encounter?"

"Winston, I leave nothing to chance."

I smiled. That was Harry.

"You will help, won't you?" Harry asked. He reinforced his request with a gaze as sharp as his clothes.

"Of course," I sighed.

"Good. I knew you wouldn't let me down. Winston, you're one of the few people in this world today that I can count on. I'll send Caroline to see you. Where are you staying?"

"At the Kensington Park Hotel."

"A hotel?"

I shrugged.

"I hear it's a nice one," Harry said.

"Very accommodating."

So here I was, strolling into the lobby of the Kensington Park Hotel to meet Caroline Avalon. I found her sitting in one of the comfortable chairs surrounding the comfortable fireplace.

"Caroline," I said.

She turned and rose from the chair. Her gray business suit was impeccably tailored, her dark blue neck scarf unmistakably silk, her posture irresistibly sensual. Style, you either have it, or you don't, and if you have it you have it all the time. Caroline Avalon had it, and she had it all the time. She was a real *femme d'affaire*.

I watched her hurry toward me. Her desperate hug nearly creased my suit. The poor girl was a bit rattled, so I did the gentlemanly thing and quickly poured two glasses of sherry.

"Caroline, what's wrong?" I asked.

"That annoying Halzbee followed me here. He made some awful threats and tried to bully me. That man is a real brute." Her eyes narrowed, and her lips tightened.

"Your father doesn't care much for him either."

"I'm so glad Daddy ran into you." She smiled softly. "It's given him some hope. But I'm afraid I don't share his optimism. I don't doubt your ability, Winston, but Halzbee's position is too strong."

She lowered her head. I placed a finger under her chin and raised it.

"Never give up hope, Caroline."

"It's been a long time since I've seen you." She took my hand. She had that nostalgic look in her eyes, the kind of look Hollywood has made a fortune from.

"Yes, it has," I said.

"I heard you spent some time in South America," she said.

"Yes, I did." I wondered where she had heard that.

"I always wondered what had happened to you. You just…"

I moved my finger from under her chin to her lips. Some things should be kept in the past.

"Let's focus on the job at hand, shall we?"

She returned my smile and let go of my hand. I led her back to the fireplace.

"Do you know anything about business, Winston? Do you really think you can help?"

"Helping people is my business," I said.

The crackling fire provided a polyrhythmic counterpoint to the clinking of our sherry glasses.

*   *   *

"James, Harry may or may not be right about Halzbee's extortion." I settled into a comfortable, antique armchair built in a more comfortable, antique era. "Harry is a fine gentleman, but he's also strong-willed and used to getting his way."

"Yes, sir. The possibility exists that he is exaggerating the matter to serve his own desires."

"I suppose the prudent thing to do would be to test Halzbee and confirm it for ourselves."

"Yes, that would be very prudent, sir."

"Even if Halzbee hasn't done anything illegal, if he gets control of Avalon Industries, innocent people will lose their jobs. Halzbee will profit while others suffer. James, we cannot let that happen."

"No, sir."

"But it's quite a fix. Even if Halzbee makes only a buck profit on each share, he would still pocket $2 million. Harry figures Halzbee's financing cost is twelve dollars a share, and that means he could offer up to $77 a share and still make that $2 million."

"If he lowers his financing costs, he would be able to offer even more or make an even greater profit," James said.

"If the deal stays as it is, he will net a cool eight mil. He doesn't have much incentive to look for better financing."

"He would if someone else entered the bidding."

I looked at James with that look of amazement that I give him when he says something amazing.

"Yes, James, I suppose that would be an incentive."

"It may also help determine the extent of Mr. Halzbee's extortion, if any."

"Sort of like killing two birds with one stone."

"Yes, sir.

Good chauffeur, that James. Do you know how hard? No, you probably don't.

*   *   *

"What the hell's this?" Harry roared. He slammed the Wall Street Journal onto the table. I assumed he was referring to the story about Winston Churchill offering $76 a share for Avalon Industries. Caroline quietly sat next to him and did not look at me.

"Are you trying to buy our -- I mean Caroline's -- company? What do you want with Avalon Industries? I asked you to save the company, not take it over yourself."

"But Harry..."

"I thought I could trust you. This is my reward for that trust?" He grabbed the newspaper and shook it in my face. "And after I got you that big house for the party you're going to throw."

He rose and grabbed Caroline's hand. She looked at me with moist eyes.

"But Harry…"

"Don't 'but Harry' me. Come on, Caroline, let's go."

He left in a huff, dragging Caroline with him.

*   *   *

Harry eventually calmed down and attended my party. The party was to be Halzbee's first test. Harry arrived with Caroline on his arm. His tux had seen a few too many social gatherings, but he still looked dapper. Bespoke clothing is always an indication of true and lasting style.

Caroline was smashing. Her hair was Hollywood, her frock French, her aura alluring.

"What are you up to, Winston?" Harry asked.

"I'm trying to save Avalon Industries."

"How, by buying it yourself?"

"Relax, Harry. Trust me."

"And how can you afford to make an offer of $76 a share? Where's your money coming from? Are you making a deal with someone else?"

"Relax, Harry. Enjoy the party, and don't worry about what

I'm doing."

"Enjoy the party? How can I enjoy the party when my -- I mean Caroline's -- company is about to be taken over? To tell you the truth, I wouldn't be here if she hadn't dragged me along. I was pretty upset with you. In fact, I still am to a certain extent."

I turned to Caroline.

"I'm glad you brought him. Maybe it will soften him up."

Harry grumbled and filled his mouth with champagne.

"Do you know all of these people?" Caroline asked.

"Most of them. They're professional party-goers. The city is full of them. They come in useful when I need to throw a bash like this. I just order them when I order the party supplies."

Caroline laughed. It was good to see her laugh. She hadn't done much of that lately. Her laughing abruptly stopped when Halzbee appeared.

"Well, well, well, look who's here: Harry Avalon and his lovely daughter." It was the flamboyant man with the new Rolls I had seen leaving the Kensington Park Hotel before I met with Caroline. He was wearing a pale yellow suit with a blue open collar university-striped shirt. Can you believe it! A man who dresses that poorly must be stopped on no other grounds other than his crimes against sartorial decency.

"Halzbee! Who invited you?" Harry yelled.

"Actually, I did," I said.

"Churchill!" Harry screamed. "You've gone too far this time! Inviting this buzzard to your party goes way beyond reason."

Caroline's face dropped.

"Avalon, old man, don't get so annoyed," Halzbee said.

"Why did you come over here?" Harry growled. "What do you want?"

"Avalon Industries, of course!" he laughed. His face turned into soft clay and slowly transformed into a giant grin. It was the kind of face you'd like to blow smoke into if you smoked.

"By the way," I said. "I'm your host, Winston Churchill." I extended a hand toward Halzbee.

Halzbee laughed again, louder and more animated than before.

"Winston Churchill?" he said. He took a cigar from his vest pocket and did a poor imitation of the former British Prime Minister.

"Not that Winston Churchill," I said. "I'm the other Winston Churchill, the one offering $76 a share for Avalon Industries."

Halzbee stopped laughing. He chewed the end of his unlit cigar, rocked on the heels of his feet, and stared at me. He stuck out his chin and looked down the end of his nose. "So," was all he said. He then spun on his heels, and he was gone.

Harry watched him leave, then turned to me.

"What's the idea of inviting that buzzard to the party?" he asked.

"I wanted to meet him," I said.

"There are other ways to meet him," Harry growled.

"Yes, why taunt him and make him mad?" Caroline asked.

"I have my reasons," I smiled. "Enjoy the party," I said then I was gone.

*   *   *

Sometimes one must stir up a hornet's nest at the risk of getting stung. The morning papers reported Halzbee's new offer of $77 a share. I had stirred the hornet's nest, all right. Of course, one can't let these things die down. A little more stirring is always in order.

"James, prepare the Rolls."

"Yes, sir."

The evening was cool but clear. It was time to give Halzbee his second test. I slipped on a dark gray wool overcoat and added a tan cashmere scarf. Even stirring up trouble requires the proper attire.

A little bird had told me that Halzbee would be dining at Amelio's, an expensive restaurant frequented by patrons who had something to prove. What Halzbee had already established was his absolute lack of sartorial flair. I found him consuming a multi-course dinner in the company of a portable telephone and a little bird of his own. His suit was even more hideous than the awful yellow thing he had worn to my party. No matter how hard you try, you will never make a plaid sports coat over contrasting plaid trousers look like anything but a clown's costume. Style, never mind…

"Halzbee, old man," I said. I pulled a chair up to his table, careful not to get too close to that sports coat. The maitre d' approached, but James intervened and prevented him from interfering. Good chauffeur, that James.

"Well, it's Churchill, isn't it? You are an annoying little gadfly, aren't you?" His sardonic grin was intended to impress his companion, but she was much too interested in James to notice. "You have by now seen my latest offer for Avalon Industries."

"Yes, but I'm sure you have not yet seen mine." I pulled a press release from my coat pocket. "The way I figure it, you can't profitably offer more than $77 a share for Avalon Industries."

You could almost hear Halzbee's brain calculating.

"That's why tomorrow I will offer $78 a share."

His face turned the color of molten lava then the rest of him erupted.

"What are you doing!" he screamed. "You can't possibly make any money at $78 a share!"

"I can if my financing costs are significantly lower than yours are."

"What? That's impossible. No one can beat my deals, no one!"

"Be seeing you, old man." I gave him a little pat on the arm with the press release and sauntered off. I saw him grab his phone as I walked out the door. Who would he be calling at this hour?

James, having taken care of the maitre d', waited by the Rolls. He opened the door, and I climbed into the leather-encased back seat. James closed the door and slid behind the wheel.

"Home, James."

The Rolls rolled smoothly down Powell Street and onto Columbus Avenue, the main artery of San Francisco's Italian flavored North Beach neighborhood. As we approached the Financial District, James spent an unusual amount of time looking into the rearview mirror.

"See someone you know?" I asked.

"Someone I do not know," he replied.

"Then I think we should make their acquaintance."

He was able to keep the look of delight from his face, but he could not keep it from his eyes.

"Yes, sir."

He tightened his seat belt and steered for a safer part of the city. The long and vacant streets near the city's southern piers were perfect. The car behind us followed, and when we crossed the bridge onto Army Street, James pushed the accelerator to the floor.

Now let me tell you, a Rolls Royce is not a high-performance automobile. It was built for quiet, effortless motorway touring, not nipping and tucking through S-curves at 2g's. James kept the accelerator on the floorboard, and the Rolls accelerated mildly, perturbed at having been asked to perform such a barbaric task.

James turned off the headlights. The tires yelped like wounded dogs as he coaxed the Rolls through a hard left turn and then a right. The sudden turns caught our pursuers by surprise, and James had to slow down to avoid losing them. He stopped in front of a dismal warehouse with stained brick walls. Tall weeds grew along a rusting chain-link fence, and the wind squealed through the broken windowpanes. I emerged from the Rolls and waited in front of the building.

A dark blue Mercedes sedan slid to a rock-throwing halt. Both front doors opened. The driver stayed next to the car; the man from the passenger seat took giant strides toward me. The Mercedes' headlights were still on, and all I saw was the man's silhouette.

"What can I do for you?" I asked him.

"Just shut up and listen. I have some business advice for you."

"Free advice?"

"Don't get smart. You just drop your offer for Avalon Industries."

"That doesn't sound very smart."

"It's a bad deal."

"Bad for whom?"

"For you." The man was now close enough to be seen clearly. His head looked as if it had been molded inside a football helmet. He certainly didn't look much like a businessman.

"Tell Halzbee he should take his own advice," I said.

The eyes in his football head became baseballs.

"Don't look so surprised," I said. "Only two people are interested in Avalon Industries other than me: Harry Avalon and Halzbee. Harry Avalon wouldn't use strongarm tactics to discourage me. That leaves only your boss, Halzbee."

"You're too smart for your own good," the football head said.

"It's all this free advice I'm getting."

He stepped forward but stopped when he heard a muffled whimper coming from near his car. He turned, stared into the headlights, then took a few tentative steps toward the Mercedes. There was a lump on the ground, and it was his partner. Before he realized what was happening, James was on him.

"Hey!"

"Tell Halzbee I appreciate his advice," I said to the man as he struggled against James' hold. "But a little competition never hurt anyone."

"It's going to hurt you," he grunted.

I smiled. James tossed the man toward the Mercedes, and he

stumbled over his partner and fell to the ground.

I straightened my tie and adjusted my pocket square. Style, you either have it, or you don't, and if you have it you have it all the time.

"Home, James."

*   *   *

"Harry was right about Halzbee's strongarm tactics," I said to James.

"Yes, sir."

"How childish."

"Very."

"It's time to teach this chap a lesson," I said. "Clown suit and all."

"Indeed, sir."

"It's time to do some fishing, and I've got just the bait."

I settled into a cozy study and went to work on a letter, a letter all about financing acquisitions. I typed it on letterhead stationery that once belonged to a banker I had encountered.

"Ready, James?" I asked.

"Yes, sir," he said, looking a bit too physically fit for an investment banker. However, he did carry an air of authority.

"Here's the letter. You know what to do."

"Yes, sir."

Fishing is a sport for the patient. Just because you have the right bait doesn't mean you'll catch anything. Besides, fish can sense tension, and they'll stay well away from nervous fishermen. It's best to wait calmly.

I waited calmly with a Bass Ale.

*   *   *

"Winston, you've let me down." Harry Avalon was not happy. "I've learned that Halzbee will offer $79 a share at tomorrow's Avalon Industries shareholder's meeting. I don't know how he can afford to pay that much and still make an acceptable profit. He must have gotten a better deal from his banker. But that's a dollar a share more than you're offering. That may not seem like much, but it is to those who own thousands of shares. Our only hope is that the shareholders won't go for it."

"But they will, Daddy," Caroline said. "Wouldn't you? I'm afraid it's hopeless."

Harry hugged his daughter.

"I guess we've lost the company, no thanks to you," he snapped. He stared at me, then turned away.

"But Harry..."

But he was gone.

*   *   *

The Avalon Industries shareholder's meeting attracted a great deal of attention. The rumor of Halzbee's sweetened takeover bid had enticed nearly every shareholder to attend. A large flock of reporters, smelling a good story, roosted among the crowd.

Halzbee nested in the front row. At least he wasn't wearing that hideous yellow suit. Instead, he was a picture of corporate sartorial boredom: a solid navy-blue suit, white shirt, and red tie. Traditional, but oh so uninspiring. And no pocket square. I mean, really!

James waited out of sight just outside the back door. I strolled down an aisle and sat next to Harry. He barely acknowledged my presence. I nodded to Halzbee, who was only a dozen seats away. He smiled like a man with emotional problems and gave me a childlike wave. Harry simmered like boiling chili.

Caroline called the meeting to order. She was very nervous. Not good for fishing. Her strong public speaking skills abandoned her, and her voice quivered, and her eyes darted about.

Halzbee had used his clout as a major shareholder to bully his way onto the agenda and was given the floor after the conclusion of routine business. He took the stage and stood behind the podium.

"It's good to see so many of you here," he said. His shiny gray-blonde hair glimmered under the lights. "I promise to make your attendance worth your while."

He paused. I assumed he thought he was adding to the drama. He wasn't.

"I'm sure you are all aware of the recent offer of $78 a share for Avalon Industries stock," he snickered. "Peanuts, I say. You deserve more, and you shall get more. Therefore, I hereby make an offer of $79 a share for Avalon Industries common stock."

The audience rustled, and a dull roar drifted across the room. Halzbee stood at the podium and treated the roar as applause. When things had sufficiently quieted down, I stood up. Someone handed me a microphone.

"That Avalon Industries shareholders are deserving is beyond question," I said. "That is why they deserve to know more about your offer."

Halzbee squinted. The stage lights prevented him from clearly seeing the audience.

"What would you like to know about my offer?" he asked.

"For a start, where are you getting your financing?"

Halzbee arrogantly stuck his hands into his trouser pockets. Only his thumbs showed.

"I have very strong financial backing," he said.

"And where is that coming from?"

"The West Coast Commercial Bank," Halzbee beamed.

"Really?" I displayed my best "I'm puzzled" look.

Halzbee then recognized my voice, and cracks of concern began to show on his arrogant face.

"What's wrong with that?" he asked.

"Nothing," I said.

"Well, then," Halzbee said.

"Who is your banker?" I asked.

"Mr. Richard Rigger, Senior Vice-President, if that's any of your business."

I plastered bewilderment on my face the way a builder plasters drywall. The shareholders next to me became curious. The reporters smelled blood and circled the waters.

"It's everyone's business because Richard Rigger has not worked for the West Coast Commercial Bank for several months," I said. "I believe he's now in the Peace Corps or something like that."

The crowd rumbled.

"That's impossible," Halzbee said. "I met with him yesterday."

"I don't know who you met with, but it certainly wasn't Richard Rigger. He's no longer an investment banker."

"How do you know?" Halzbee challenged.

"A phone call to the bank will confirm it."

A louder roar filled the room. Cameras flashed. Reporters dashed from the room to call the West Coast Commercial Bank. Halzbee was stunned. Caroline quickly adjourned the meeting, and the press descended upon Halzbee like locusts.

"This is your doing, I assume," Harry said.

I smiled.

"Damn good," he said. "I knew all along you wouldn't let me down."

*   *   *

The next day I met Caroline for lunch. We dined outdoors at Enrico's.

"I'm so glad we could have lunch," she said. That nostalgic look returned to her eyes.

"It's my pleasure," I said.

"Have you seen today's Journal?" she asked.

"No, I haven't."

She handed me the paper and pointed to a headline: "Halzbee Drops Avalon Industries Bid; Churchill Follows Suit."

"Daddy says you were responsible for this. Is it true?"

I rose as James pulled my Rolls to a stop in front of the restaurant.

"Let me give you a word of advice, Caroline."

"And what's that, Winston?"

"Don't ever come to me for financing."

We smiled. I kissed her on the forehead and climbed into the Rolls.

"Home, James."

6 THE ROGUE'S QUIET WEEKEND

The hardest part of thwarting an unscrupulous financier's hostile takeover attempt is recovering one's energy once the thwarting is complete. The deed itself is challenging and tiring. Offer, counter-offer. Bluff, counter-bluff. Perhaps even a little bit of deception. When the stakes are high, the ethical standards are low. It's enough to drain the old *joie de vie* and make you feel as if you had just spent the last 24 hours traversing the French countryside behind the wheel of a D-type Jaguar. A quiet weekend is typically required to restore one's passion for *le grand monde*.

My preferred destination for a quiet weekend is always California's Gold Country. The abandoned mines of the Sierra Nevada foothills calm one's soul, and the stately homes filled with ghosts of the Gold Rush fortify one's spirit. So, it was off to Nevada City with high hopes and high expectations.

*　　*　　*

"James," I said. "This is not what I had expected."

"No, sir."

I had not expected to find every parking space on Broad Street filled with an expensive automobile. It was worse than watching a sure thing stumble down the backstretch. And you know how bad that is, don't you?

"Look, James," I said. "There are Jags and Mercedes everywhere."

"A few Rollers, as well," he said.

Tasteless new ones, of course. Their ostentatious owners were no doubt lurking about wherever it is that ostentatious owners lurk. All very distressing. Broad Street, Nevada City, is not supposed to look like Rodeo Drive, Beverly Hills.

"See if you can find a parking space."

"Yes, sir."

After several tours of Broad Street, a spot finally opened up in front of the National Hotel, a brick building with tall, white wooden columns and white, intricately carved wooden balconies. It was a nice place to park a classic Rolls Royce.

James nudged the Rolls to within inches of a ragged, dark brown Peugeot 504 station wagon, the only unpretentious car on the street.

"Well done, James." Good chauffeur, that James. Do you know how hard it is to find a chauffeur named James? No, you probably don't.

"Thank you, sir." He silently slid out of the Rolls and very properly opened my door. In case you're interested, I was wearing a yellow ascot tucked into a blue silk shirt and a white linen suit. A Panama hat completed what, in my opinion, is the perfect holiday look. Some may regard it as too Hollywood, but a classic becomes a classic for a reason. And I'm sure I've told you before that when one owns a Rolls Royce, one's wardrobe must measure up, even while vacationing.

Our exit from the Rolls rustled an elderly couple from the Peugeot. They were a friendly-looking pair in British-style clothes that were worn at the edges. A wedge-shaped driving hat rested precariously on top of the man's head, and a thin, gray mustache clung to his upper lip. Surprisingly dashing. The woman's gray curls dangled from the type of hat worn by butterfly collectors.

"Nice automobile," the man said, admiring the beautifully anachronistic lines of my Silver Cloud III.

"Thank you," I said.

"I don't see many like that anymore."

"No, one doesn't,"

"What year is it?"

"1963."

He nodded and stepped back for a more panoramic view.

"Mr. Jepson has invited so many wealthy people here that we feel a bit out of place," the woman said.

I looked at James. Neither of us had a clue as to who Mr. Jepson was.

"You must be very wealthy to drive a car like that," the man said.

"Do not be deceived by appearances," I smiled.

"Well, we're happy just to have the chance to hobnob with the rich and famous," the woman smiled. Her lovely face reminded me of toasted bread and warm honey.

"It's a wonderful opportunity, don't you think?" her husband said.

"Yes," I said. "I suppose it is." I exchanged another glance with James, and he raised his eyebrows.

"I can't believe so many people have turned out," the man continued, nodding at the row of expensive cars. "I had no idea so many people read this paper." He took a thin newspaper from under his arm.

"Oh, *The California Investment News*," I said. None of my business acquaintances cared much for that particular publication. Then again, none of them drove old Peugeots.

"I guess it just goes to show you what a good deal Mr. Jepson is offering us," the man said.

I was beginning to wonder about this Jepson fellow, and you know how I get when I get to wondering.

"May I buy you a cup of coffee?" I asked.

"Yes, indeed!" he said. The old man smiled at his wife.

James stayed with the Rolls while I led the couple into the cafe of the National Hotel.

"I'm Winston Churchill," I said, shaking the man's hand.

"By Jove!" He gave me an astonished look. "You're not related to **the** Winston Churchill, are you?" He squinted at me.

"No, no relation," I said.

"My name's Ansley Duke," he said.

"And I'm Mary Queen of Scots," his wife added.

"She's not really," Ansley growled.

"But my real name is Mary, and I am glad to meet you, Mr. Churchill." Her smile was as soft as billowy clouds. "I hope my little joke didn't put you off. Is your name really Winston Churchill?"

"It is, and a little humor is not wasted on me."

"I'm glad," she said. Her toast and honey look reappeared.

"We'll have tea instead of coffee if you don't mind," Ansley said.

"I don't mind at all," I said. Someday, I will write a treatise on the personality differences between tea and coffee drinkers. Keep an eye out for it.

"Where are you from?" I asked.

"Berkeley," Mary said.

In case you don't know, Berkeley is a university town across the Bay from San Francisco. It's a little world of its own, full of cultural diversity, unconventional thinking, and good intentions. It's also close to the horse racing at Golden Gate Fields.

"What do you do for a living?" I asked.

"We're teachers," Ansley said.

"College teachers," Mary added. "Professors."

"Naturally. How did you become readers of *The California Investment News*?" I asked.

Ansley placed the newspaper on the table.

"A colleague told us about it," he said. "We've subscribed to it for quite a few years. We've never invested in any of its recommendations, though. Seems frivolous to spend so much money subscribing to something we never use. To tell you the truth, we've always been afraid to invest in anything. We've always been conservative, putting our money into our savings account at the bank. We've let opportunities pass us by. But we're not going to let it happen again. We're tired of missing out on great investments."

"Yes," Mary said. "I guess we have been a bit stodgy with our money."

"But you still have it," I said. "There is something to be said for fiscal conservatism."

"Yes, I suppose you're right," Ansley shrugged. "But it's time for us to be more aggressive. After all, we're not young anymore. We won't have many more opportunities like this one. Have you decided which parcel you're going to buy?"

"I'm afraid I didn't come here to transact business," I said. "I'm vacationing."

"Vacationing?" Ansley's mustache thickened. "But your car, I thought for sure..." He turned to his wife.

"As Mr. Churchill said, do not be deceived by appearances."

"Oh," Ansley swallowed hard. "You see, this investment opportunity is secret, and I shouldn't have told you as much as I have."

"You have told me nothing of consequence," I said.

"It's invitation-only," Ansley continued. "Invitations were sent only to long-time subscribers of *The California Investment News*."

"You don't have to say anymore," I said.

"Well, it's a new Gold Rush," Ansley continued. "Of course, if you haven't received an invitation from Mr. Jepson, we shouldn't tell you about it."

"You needn't say another word. I respect your privacy."

"But I think we can trust Mr. Churchill, don't you, Mary?" He looked at his wife and then at me. "You won't tell anybody, will you?"

"Mum's the word."

Ansley reached into his tweed sport coat and pulled out a clump of papers, and he passed them on to me as if he were passing on state secrets.

"The prospectus," he whispered.

I opened it and read about the deal. Two hundred parcels of land were for sale with a limit of five parcels per investor. A detailed map indicated the location of each parcel and its selling price. One of the parcels was circled.

The prospectus also contained a market forecast written by a company named International Investments. The forecast detailed the plans of the Davidson Development Corporation to build an office park and a luxury hotel next to the property. A Davidson Development spokesman listed the area's proximity to the ski slopes of Lake Tahoe and the gambling of Reno, Nevada, as reasons for building in the Nevada City area. Those benefits, it was stated, would attract the necessary tenants.

"You're going to buy the circled parcel?" I asked.

"Yes, that's right," Ansley said. "You see, those development plans haven't been made public yet, and when they are, land in this area will be worth a fortune."

"Especially the land next to the development," Mary said.

"That's the land Mr. Jepson is selling."

Ansley looked around the cafe. It was two-thirds empty. One other patron sipped coffee and slurped pancakes at a table on the other side of the room.

"I'm just looking to make sure Mr. Jepson isn't here," he said. "He spends quite a bit of time in the cafe. He wouldn't appreciate our telling you about the deal."

"Who is Mr. Jepson?" I asked.

"Why, he's the publisher of *The California Investment News*."

"Oh."

Ansley turned pensive.

"You know, it sure was nice of Mr. Jepson to send us a personal invitation," he said. "I didn't think he even knew we read his newsletter. So many important people subscribe to it that I didn't think he would bother with us. We don't have that much money. Oh, we have enough to buy one parcel of land, but that's all. It was so nice of Mr. Jepson to include us in his select list of potential investors."

"Yes," Mary said. "It was very civil of him. It shows that you don't have to drive a Rolls Royce or be Mary Queen of Scots to be taken into Mr. Jepson's confidence."

I smiled and gave the prospectus back to Ansley.

"Don't you find it odd that Mr. Jepson is selling his land?" I asked. "If it's going to be so valuable, why isn't he keeping it for himself?"

"That's the typical response." Ansley stiffened and sat back in his chair. "Mr. Jepson warned us of that. But you see, he's not greedy, Mr. Churchill. He's going to keep some of the parcels for himself and sell the rest of them. He mentioned something about taxes that I didn't fully understand, but his main reason for selling is to reward all of us who have been faithful subscribers to his newsletter."

"He's being very charitable," Mary added. Her smile was thin. She blinked and took a sip of her tea.

"Yes, very charitable," I said. "Still, one shouldn't rush into such things," I said.

"Oh, we won't," Ansley said. "We have until two o'clock tomorrow afternoon to make our decision."

"That's not much time."

"One must move fast in business," Ansley said. "They are going to announce the development plans on Monday. If we don't buy now, it will be too late. Once the plans have been made public, the value of the land will skyrocket, and we will have missed out on the chance of a lifetime. Opportunities are fleeting."

"Oh, Ansley," Mary laughed. "You sound like a TV commercial."

Ansley blushed and shrugged.

"Has anyone verified the market forecast?" I asked.

"Mr. Churchill," Ansley frowned. "I'm sure there's no need for that. There's no reason to question Mr. Jepson's integrity. We've read his newsletter for quite some time. When Mr. Jepson says it's a good deal, I believe him. You aren't jealous, are you?"

"Sorry, just my suspicious nature." It was time to change the subject. "Where are you staying?" I asked.

"Here in the hotel," Mary said. "You know, it's the oldest continuously operating hotel in California."

"I didn't know that."

"Where are you staying?" Ansley asked.

"In a private house." I tried to remain nonchalant. As usual, the house did not belong to me, and I hadn't exactly been invited to stay in it.

"Oh, that must be nice," Mary said. She clasped her hands together and smiled. "There are such beautiful homes here."

"Yes. We're going to buy one with the money we make off this real estate deal," Ansley said.

"Yes, we've always wanted a Victorian," Mary added.

"I'm sure you'll be pleased with it," I said. I reached for the check.

"Oh, we'll pay for that, Mr. Churchill," Ansley said, grabbing the check. "We might as well get used to spending a little money."

"Thank you," I said. "I've enjoyed your company."

"It's been our pleasure." Ansley shook my hand.

"Goodbye, Mr. Churchill," Mary said.

I nodded and returned to the Rolls. James opened the rear door, and I slid into the back seat.

"Is something wrong, sir?" James asked.

"I'm not sure."

I told him of Jepson's real estate deal.

"Very unusual, sir."

"Yes. Jepson's charity worries me. It's not that I don't believe in the basic goodness of mankind or anything like that; it's simply that basic goodness seldom has a place in business the way most people conduct it."

"Indeed, sir."

"If this real estate deal is a scam, many people will lose a lot of money."

"Quite likely."

"Of course, I don't care what happens to the wealthy folks with the expensive cars."

"One should not."

"But the Dukes are nice people."

"I'm sure they are, sir."

"And they are not wealthy. Someone should look after their interests."

"Certainly, sir."

"I suppose if we don't do it, no one will."

"Then I take it the quiet weekend is over?" James asked.

I leaned back and adjusted my ascot.

"To the hunt, James!"

*   *   *

I figured if Jacob Jepson were any kind of a big shot, Harry Avalon would know of him. But Harry had never heard of him nor International Investments or the Davidson Development Corporation.

"I'll do some research and call you in the morning," he said. "By the way, what's all this about? What are you up to?"

"I'm dabbling in real estate," I said.

"What?" I could almost see his perturbed face through the telephone line. "You just wait for my call." His final words were followed by a click and a dial tone.

If you know me, you know there is one thing I cannot do well, and that is wait.

"James," I said. "I think we should have a look at Jepson's property. Perhaps we can learn a few things for ourselves."

"Perhaps, sir."

"Good. Grab your Wellingtons. *La campagne* is calling!"

*　　　*　　　*

"They will have to put in roads and sewers," James said as he surveyed the area. "Have they filed an environmental impact study?"

"I didn't see one mentioned in the prospectus," I said.

James stopped the Rolls. We put on our Wellingtons and hiked through tall grass until we came to another small clearing. We were surprised to find a raggedy shack with smoke rising from its flimsy chimney. An old man sat on a tree stump in front of the shack. He was cleaning a large hunting knife with a dirty rag. His prickly beard and sandblasted hair covered his face. Only his eyes were visible. It made him resemble a porcupine.

"Hello," I said.

The man looked up, squinted, and rose from the stump. His eyebrows twitched with suspicion. James kept an eye on the knife.

"Howdy," he said.

We ventured a few steps closer.

"Nice knife," I said.

The man looked at his knife.

"Mighty fine huntin' knife, that is." He held it up so we could see it better. "Used to belong to my father. He skinned quite a few bears with it."

"Bears?" I looked at James.

"Now, don't get nervous, mister. Not around here, up in Washington State."

"Oh," I said. "I don't suppose you see many bears around here."

"No, and I don't usually see many folks either," the man replied.

"Well, you're going to be seeing many more of them pretty soon," I said.

"What do you mean?" He squinted again.

"Do you live here?" I asked.

"Yup." He tilted his head and stopped squinting. "You got a problem with that?"

"No, not at all. But you don't own this land, do you?"

"Nobody owns this land, mister. Nobody wants it."

"Well, someone wants it now."

The old man twitched again.

"Do you own this land?" he asked. He tilted his head in the other direction and looked at me with half-closed eyes.

"No, I don't own it. What's your name?"

"Emery."

"What do you do around here, Emery?"

"I used to pan for gold," he said. His suspicious eyes opened and closed.

"Gold?"

"Now, don't get excited, mister. There ain't none anymore. Used to be plenty of it. Not here, up by the river, little ways up north. I panned more gold than you've probably ever seen. I remember those days. We'd strike gold and then rush off to the National Hotel and buy everyone drinks. Those were good days, mister. Drank quite a bit. But them days are gone, and they won't come back. No sir, mister, there ain't no more gold here."

"How do you know? Maybe the gold's underground?"

"Listen, mister; I can smell gold. I can take a hand full of dirt, bring it up to my nose, and smell if there's gold down below." He reached down for a handful of soil, brought it to his nose, sniffed, shook his head, and dropped the dirt. "Nope, no gold here."

"Very scientific," I said.

"Science ain't got nothing to do with it," he snapped.

"I see."

"Mister, I've smelled every bit of land in this county, and there ain't no gold here. Not here, not in the river. None, nowhere. There ain't no gold nowhere around here."

"Then why are you still here?"

"I ain't doing no prospecting if that's what you mean. Oh, I go down to the river every now and then, but it ain't no good. I live off the gold I panned fifty years ago."

"Well, there's new gold on its way, Emery," I said. "Someone's going to build offices and hotels on this land. "

"Offices? Hotels? Why would anybody want to build those things here?" He looked around the rough land. "This land's worthless, mister. That's why nobody cares if I live here."

"I'm afraid those days are over, Emery."

*　　*　　*

"James, we need an airplane."

"Sir?"

"Harry Avalon may be on to something, but he needs more information, and that information happens to be under lock and key."

"I see, sir."

"He needs to utilize some of your more practical skills to obtain the information."

"Very good, sir."

"But we don't have much time. I'm beginning to think Jepson's deal is a scam, and if it is, we'll have to be back before two o'clock to prevent Mr. and Mrs. Duke from losing their life savings."

"And if it is not a scam?"

"Then I guess we'll relax and enjoy the flight."

We drove to the local airport at a speed that was slightly uncomfortable for the Rolls. The sun was still rising, and the only sign of life was a sleepy tabby on top of an old oil barrel. We borrowed an airplane and flew to San Francisco. Harry met us at the airport.

"What are you doing in Nevada City?" Harry asked.

"Having a quiet weekend."

"That's what I was having until you called." He looked me over in that special way he has of looking people over. "I suppose I owe you one, though. Come on." He led us to his car.

"What have you discovered?" I asked.

"Listen, Winston. I'm not sure. I may have found something, but I need more information, and that information isn't at my immediate disposal."

"You shall have it," I said.

Harry stopped his Mercedes at the fringes of the Financial District just a few blocks from the offices of International Investments. James slid out of the car and immediately went to work. He did his usual superb job and obtained the information without a hitch.

"I don't want to know how you got that," Harry said, nodding toward the bundle of papers in James' arms. "But it was a damn fine job."

I smiled. Harry drove us back to his spectacular Russian Hill home, and we settled into a den that housed more books than most municipal libraries. Several vintage first editions shared shelf space with law books and business tomes. He took a bottle of port from a wine rack that someone had ingeniously built into an antique glass-doored bookcase. The port was a 1963 vintage from the Rio Torto valley. It had a fine color, fine nose, and a fine taste.

We toasted each other, then Harry sat down and examined the papers James had obtained for him.

"It's a very complicated scheme," he said after a while. "There are so many holding companies involved that it's hard to follow. But it boils down to this: two men named Jacob Jepson and Ernie Davidson run the entire show. Look," Harry said, pointing at some diagrams he had drawn. "At the top, we have Ernie Davidson and Jacob Jepson. Each of them owns 50% of West Coast Construction, and West Coast Construction owns 50% of Davidson Development and also 75% of International Investments."

"The firm that did the market forecast," James said.

'Correct. Jacob Jepson owns the other 25% of International Investments, and he also owns all of *The California Investment News*."

"What about the other 50% of Davidson Development?" I asked.

"*The California Investment News* owns it."

"What? Harry, you're talking in riddles."

"I'm talking in riddles because this entire business is a riddle," he grumbled. Harry never did have much patience with financial neophytes. "What it all means is this: Ernie Davidson and Jacob Jepson own everything. They own the company that did the market forecast, and they own the firm that is supposed to do the development. They also own the newsletter that is providing them with investors."

"Shady," I said.

"Shady? It's more than shady. Now listen to this. The important part is the history of these firms. West Coast Construction has embarked upon several other developments recently, each time using different holding companies. Each time nothing was built. In fact, as far as I can tell, West Coast Construction has never constructed anything, and Davidson Development has never developed anything. In all cases, International Investments did the market forecast. Several lawsuits have already been filed against them in other States. Listen, Winston, these men are crooks. What you've got here is a scam."

"I was afraid of that," I said. "That's bad news for the Dukes."

"Who?"

"Never mind. You don't know them. Anyway, thanks for the analysis, Harry. May I take these papers?"

"Sure."

"Now, if you'd take us back to the airport, we have to be back in Nevada City before two o'clock."

Harry looked at his watch.

"Good luck," he said. "You haven't a chance in hell."

*   *   *

Harry was right. It was 2:15 by the time James brought the Rolls to a halt in front of the National Hotel. I did not wait for him to open my door. Ansley and Mary sat at a table in the cafe.

"Mr. Churchill," Ansley called. He looked like a teenage boy who had just received his first kiss. "Where have you been?"

"In San Francisco."

"San Francisco? What were you doing there?"

Mary looked at me funny.

"Did you buy that land?" I asked.

"Yes, of course," he said. "So did many others. You should have seen them all, Mr. Churchill!" His mustache twitched with self-satisfied excitement.

My heart sank to the floor, and I sat down to join it.

"You don't look too well, Mr. Churchill," Mary said. "Is something wrong?"

"I'm afraid I have some bad news for you."

Mary tightened, and her face lost its toast and honey look.

"Oh?" she said.

"I went to San Francisco to investigate Mr. Jepson and the companies involved in his real estate deal."

"What? Mr. Churchill, you didn't?" Ansley was a mixture of anger and surprise.

"What did you find, Mr. Churchill?" Mary asked. She clasped her hands tightly together.

I placed Harry's papers on the table.

"Unfortunately, Jepson's real estate deal is a scam," I said. "Jepson and his partner are crooks. They are very good at selling land based on phony development plans. Several lawsuits have already been filed against them. These men are frauds."

"Oh, my," Mary said. Her voice was barely a whisper.

"Are you sure?" Ansley asked. He rose and looked down at me. "You better have proof, Mr. Churchill. You just can't make accusations like that without proof."

"The proof is in these papers," I said. "With the lawsuits piling up against them, they'll probably take the money from this scam and flee the country."

Ansley sat down and looked at the papers and then stared into space. Reality hit him like the hard left hook that average boxers never see coming.

"Our entire savings," he said. "We've lost it all." His colorful face became colorless.

"We should have been more careful," Mary said. "But we were so excited."

"I'm not very excited now," Ansley moaned. They sat quietly and stared at the table. "I guess we should have listened to you, Mr. Churchill. But how were we to know?" He looked at me as his eyes pleaded his case. "We shouldn't have rushed into this. You were right."

"Oh, dear," Mary said. "Oh, dear. What should we do now? Can these men be stopped?"

"The deal will eventually be exposed for the scam that it is. You can then sue Jepson and his partner, but there will be so many other claims against them that the chances of recovering your money are not very good. And it will take time."

"Can't we call the police or some other authority?" Ansley asked.

"They haven't done anything illegal yet," I said.

"Then there's nothing we can do?" Ansley's mustache disappeared as his lips puckered.

"Nothing legal," I said.

*　　*　　*

"James, pack up the Rolls," I said. "I want to leave Nevada City as quickly as possible. This quiet weekend has been a considerable disappointment."

"Indeed, it has, sir."

We packed in silence; James then loaded the Rolls.

"To the National Hotel, James. I want to say goodbye to the Dukes."

"Yes, sir.

He drove me to the hotel then drove on to pick up a very important package. Jepson was in the hotel, taking an early supper in the cafe. He was a slovenly beast of a fellow. He wore too many gold and diamond rings and probably drove a Cadillac.

The Dukes desolately sat at a table next to the window. Have you ever seen the lost expression on hunting dogs when the fox gets away? Perhaps you haven't. Well, that expression covered the Dukes the way coastal fog covers coastal mountains.

"Hello," I said to them.

"Hello," Mary replied. Her voice was tired.

Ansley was quiet.

"Awfully decent of you to stop in and say goodbye," Mary said.

"Not at all. Actually, I'm here because I have a way to get your money back."

"What?" Ansley nearly jumped out of his chair. "By Jove, Mr. Churchill, are you serious?" Ansley looked at Mary.

"What do you intend to do?" she asked.

"I want to buy the land from you."

"Mr. Churchill," he recoiled. "We will not accept charity."

"It's not charity; it's a business deal."

"If it's not charity, then what is it?" Mary asked.

"I have a use for the land."

Ansley and Mary looked at each other.

"If you really want it, we'll sell it to you, Mr. Churchill," Ansley said. "But I don't want this to be charity."

"I don't have the money right now, but if you sign over the title to the land, I'll sign a promise to pay."

"Mr. Churchill…"

"Trust me," I said. I looked Ansley straight in the eye. "If you had listened to me the first time, you wouldn't be in this fix."

I already had the papers prepared, and I laid them on the table. We signed the agreement.

"I still don't feel right about this, Mr. Churchill," Ansley said.

Then James arrived in the Rolls, and I smiled. Ansley began to speak, but he was interrupted by Emery's appearance in the cafe.

"Wee!" Emery shouted, "Drinks for everybody!"

"Who's that, and what's he talking about?" Ansley asked.

Jepson looked up from his pork chops.

"Gold! I found gold!"

Nothing captures people's attention like gold, does it? It certainly caught Jepson's attention. He rose from his table, threw down his napkin, and approached Emery.

"Gold?" he said. His nose sniffed like a bloodhound's.

"Yup!" Emery said.

We gathered around the scruffy prospector.

"Where did you find it?" I asked.

"Right here." He pulled out a musty map and pointed to Ansley's parcel of land.

"That's my land!" Ansley said. He looked at Mary and grinned.

"No, that's my land now," I said.

Ansley's jaw dropped like a runaway elevator. His face mutated into a kaleidoscope of colors before it settled on red. You could have skated on his eyes.

"You, you, you cheated me!" he cried. "You must have known there was gold on my land! You crook! You big crook! Now you'll get the gold."

"Drinks for everyone!" Emery shouted. "Wee!"

Jepson's mouth exploded, and his eyes glazed over.

"Quiet down, would you?" he yelled.

Emery looked at Jepson.

"What for?" he asked.

"You don't want to start a stampede, do you?"

Emery blushed and shut his trap.

"No, I guess not," he whispered.

"There," Jepson nodded, wiping his forehead.

"But I'll tell you one thing," Emery continued. "That whole area's full of gold. I can smell it."

"What are you saying?" Jepson asked. He stuck out his jaw and stared at Emery.

"Look here. See there?" He pointed at the map. "There's gold there."

Jepson reeled and staggered. His porcine body swayed like a balloon in the wind.

"There's gold there?" he asked.

"You bet there is," Emery nodded.

Jepson turned to me.

"That's your land, is it?"

"It was mine," Ansley growled. James had to hold him back. It didn't take much effort. "I bought it from you this afternoon."

"Oh yes, I remember," Jepson said to Ansley.

"But I just sold it to this man." Ansley glared at me.

"Yes," I grinned. "And, thanks to the gold, that land is now worth a fortune. So is all the surrounding land."

"Mr. Jepson," Ansley said. "Didn't you know there was gold out there?"

Jepson snarled.

"No, he didn't," I said. "If he had known, he wouldn't have sold it. Now I'm going to find all the other people who bought land this weekend and buy it from them before they learn about the gold."

Jepson reeled again. You can always tell when a man is sick to his stomach by the way his skin turns color, and Jepson's skin looked like empty snakeskin. When his color returned, so did his attitude.

"You got enough money to buy all that land?" Jepson asked.

"I don't think he does," Ansley sneered. He raised his head in defiance. "He had to sign an IOU to buy my land."

"Is that right?" Jepson laughed. He had a repulsive laugh that sounded like someone banging on an empty metal barrel. "You've got to have a lot of bread to play the real estate game." He laughed again and patted me on the back. "I've got that kind of money. You don't. I can afford to buy back the land. You can't."

"Perhaps we can make a deal," I said.

"Deal? What kind of deal? You've got nothing to deal with." He had an awful grin on his chubby face.

"I've got information."

He stopped grinning.

"Once everyone learns about the gold, you'll never be able to buy back the land," I said. "At least not at a reasonable price."

"You wouldn't dare…"

I examined the pieces of gold in Emery's hand. "Excellent quality," I said.

"See that?" Emery said, pointing to one of the pieces. "That means the area's full of gold. I can tell just by looking at it. Wee! Drinks for everybody!"

"Pipe down!" Jepson yelled. "What's your deal?" he said to me.

"You buy my parcel of land, at a healthy premium, of course, and I'll keep quiet about the gold."

"That's blackmail," he said.

"Land prices will skyrocket once news of the gold gets out," I said. "My silence is worth something. It turns out you were pretty foolish to sell that land."

"Let's talk money," he said.

We settled the deal, and Jepson rushed off to buy back his land. I ushered the Duke's out of the cafe and paid them for their parcel. James waited in the Rolls.

"Mr. Churchill," Ansley said. "I don't understand it. At first, I thought you had cheated me out of my land. Then you gave me all of the money, including the extra that Jepson gave you to keep quiet about the gold. Aren't you going to keep some?"

"Yes," Mary said. "You certainly deserve a share."

"No. Take the money and put it in the bank," I said. "Return to your conservative ways."

"But you knew there was gold on that land," Ansley said. "Couldn't we have made more money if we'd kept it? Gold is precious."

I climbed into the back of the Rolls and lowered the window.

"Mr. Duke," I said as James started the engine. "The only gold on that land is fool's gold. Home, James."

7 THE ROGUE MEETS HIS MATCH

To me, she will always be the woman. I have met many women in my time, but none like Irene Atom. She was not one of those prissy, high society types who exist solely for expensive parties and pretentious paramours. No, Irene Atom was what could best be described as "clever."

* * *

It was an unusually balmy winter evening in San Francisco. The glitterati wore their fur coats out of fashion, not necessity. It was also opera season, that dangerous time of year when culture and sociality gang up on unsuspecting aspirants to the *beau monde*. I've heard that it takes a man at least six seasons to harden to the point where he can stomach the opera and still maintain enthusiasm for the post-opera party. Many do not have the mettle, and they slide back into the *bourgeoisie*, fading forever from the gossip columns.

It was Thursday night, and I was at a post-opera party in the home of a flamboyant financier. At times I may miss the opera, but I never miss the party. Unfortunately, the prima donna also had not missed the party. She artificially demurred, holding court among a group of fawning admirers. I hoped none of them would ask her to sing. It's not that I have anything against good music; it's just that there's something about sopranos. I think it's the remarkable similarity between their singing and the shrieks of love-starved cats. I crossed my fingers and hoped for the best.

"Winston!" someone called.

I turned to face the voice. It was Sidney Felstein, dashingly dressed in a stiff tuxedo with a champagne glass firmly attached to the left sleeve.

"Sidney, been to the opera, I see."

"Yes. Marvelous, simply marvelous."

The prima donna overheard our conversation and smiled.

"Don't encourage her," I muttered, pulling him aside. "So, Sidney, how have you been?"

"Fine, fine. And you?" He was nervous. Well, Sidney was always nervous. This time his nervousness was nervous.

"Fine," I said.

"Fine. Listen, Winston, I've got something to talk to you

about." He spoke softly and looked around for potential eavesdroppers.

"Fire away," I said.

"As you probably know, I've always had political ambitions."

"Is that so?"

"Yes," he nodded. "In fact, I'm running for governor next year."

"Congratulations!" I patted him on the back.

"Yes, I am quite pleased about that. But there is a dark cloud in the ointment."

"What?"

"You see, many years ago I committed a trifling indiscretion that I'm afraid might come back to haunt me. You know how the press treats electoral candidates. They rake them over the stove. They dig up all the smut they can find, regardless of how old it is."

"Yes, I suppose one must have a clean past."

"No skeletons in the cabinet."

"Right." I was beginning to worry about old Sidney. How can a man butcher so many clichés in a single conversation? Perhaps he had imbibed a bit too much of the bubbly.

"Well, I have a skeleton that must be disposed of, if you know what I mean."

"What kind of skeleton?"

He looked around again and continued once he was convinced no one could hear us.

"There are these photographs, Winston. You see, many years ago, I was romantically involved with an entertainer. The photographs are of the two of us. No one must ever see them."

"Is it so bad to have been romantically involved with an entertainer?" I asked. "Sometimes a glamorous past is an asset."

"When I say entertainer, I don't mean an artist in the traditional sense. Not a musician nor an actor."

"What do you mean, Sidney?"

"I mean an entertainer on Broadway."

"Broadway? Not bad."

"In North Beach."

"Oh, **that** Broadway." In case you don't know, Broadway in San Francisco's North Beach neighborhood was full of what can politely be called "strip joints."

"It was a clandestine relationship, and these photographs could be very damaging to my campaign if they fall into the wrong hands."

"Are you being threatened? Is she blackmailing you?"

"No." He fidgeted. "I don't think this person even knows about my plans to run for governor."

"Then what's the problem?"

"I'm afraid of the uncertainty. I'm afraid I'll be blackmailed once my candidacy is announced."

"Oh," I said.

"What I need is a preemptive strike. You know, get the photos before the temptation arises."

"I see."

"Yes, well." Sidney poured the champagne into his mouth. Words momentarily escaped him.

"And you want me to obtain these photographs for you," I said.

"Yes, Winston, that's the idea. What do you think? You can do that sort of thing, can't you?"

"What's her name?"

"Irene Atom."

"Irene Atom? I've never heard of her. Where is she living?"

"Somewhere in North Beach."

"Can you be more specific?"

"No, I can't. I haven't seen her in ages. She retired over fifteen years ago."

"That's a long time, Sidney. Are you sure she's still in The City?"

"It's not that long." He shrugged and shivered at the same time. "People have long memories."

He was holding something back, but that's just how it is with these political types.

"I suppose you're right," I said.

"Then will you help me?" he asked.

Before I could answer, my worst fears came true. The prima donna began to sing.

"Well, Sidney, I've got to go."

"But will you help me?"

"You know me, Sidney. I'm always willing to do my part to expedite the political process."

Sidney smiled. I hurried away from the party before the prima donna could inflict permanent damage to my nervous system. The only sure remedy for a soprano is the solitude of a Rolls Royce.

*   *   *

"James, I believe the best way to locate Irene Atom is to ask the North Beach old-timers."

"Indeed, sir?" He spoke in a manner that seemed to doubt my approach.

"Yes. There must be someone who knows her whereabouts. Don't you agree?"

"If you say so, sir." I found his manner a trifle annoying. I have noticed that there are times when he can be a bit arrogant. Still, he is a good chauffeur. Worth the difficulty in finding.

Despite James' doubts about my approach, I began searching for Irene Atom that evening. You've got to get up pretty late in the day if you want to find information in North Beach.

The streets glistened in the damp aftermath of a brief rain. The sudden dousing had temporarily suppressed the distinctive North Beach aromas, and they now emerged from the pores of the city and rose like steam from a baked clam. The obvious thing to do was to hit all the old joints and find someone who still knew Irene. Not quite like looking for a needle in a haystack, but almost.

James took me to Enrico's, a slowly fading North Beach icon known for live jazz and lively ambiance. I hoped to find an old-timer named Eddie Muncher, a full-time hanger-on who knew more about North Beach than any man alive. In the old days, he had owned an obscure, tiny club called "The Green Apple". Only hard-core locals ever knew of it. I kept Eddie supplied with racing tips, so he was always willing to do me a favor. And if anybody knew the whereabouts of Irene Atom, it would be Eddie Muncher.

I settled myself at an outdoor table, ordered an espresso, and watched the crowds on their way to Finocchio's next door. In case you don't know, Finocchio's was a joint specializing in female impersonators. And it was amazing how they packed them in. Mostly out-of-towners searching for a glimpse of the real San

Francisco.

But my concern wasn't the real San Francisco; it was Sidney Felstein and Irene Atom. An unlikely-sounding couple, I must say. I didn't know Sidney all that well, but it didn't surprise me that he would have gotten himself mixed up with a stripper. His taste in women was always a bit strange. Not quite gubernatorial material, if you ask me. But who's asking?

I was on my second espresso when Eddie finally wandered by. He wore a too-green plaid sport coat and a dark brown hat with a gray feather in the band. His nose had lost the battle to dominate his face, but it had not yet given up the fight.

"How ya' been, Winston?" he said.

"Good, Eddie. And you?"

"I'm still alive and kickin'."

"Still play the horses?"

"Aye, whenever I've got spare change."

I smiled and slipped a list of horses and some spare change into his coat pocket. He winked and smiled.

"Say, Eddie, I've got a question for you. "

"Ask away, Winston."

"Have you ever heard of a stripper named Irene Atom?"

"Irene Atom," he pondered. "A stripper, you say?" His eyes squinted, forehead creased, and jaw tightened. When Eddie ponders, he ponders.

"Yes," I said.

"The name sounds familiar," he said. "She still performing?"

"No. She's an old-timer. Retired at least fifteen years ago, I'm told. Thought you might have heard of her."

"My memory must be a-slippin', Winston. I don't know of no stripper named Irene Atom."

"Well, thanks for exercising your brain."

"You're welcome, Winston. I'm sorry I can't remember. I'll let you know if it comes back to me. Be seeing you." He saluted me with his index finger and shuffled off.

Have you ever noticed how interrogation makes one hungry? No, you probably haven't. Well, believe me, it does. Questioning Eddie Muncher had made me extremely hungry, so I followed the scent of garlic across the street to Original Joe's. There was nothing wrong with the food at Enrico's, but I figured I'd be able to run into a few more old-timers at Original Joe's. And I was right. I sat down at the counter next to an old hawker named Skeets.

"Hello, Skeets."

He looked at me through bangs of dry, yellow hair that was very much like the dried straw.

"Why, hello, Winston Churchill!" he said. "I haven't seen you in ages."

He held out a scruffy hand. I shook it carefully.

"How have you been?" I asked.

"Can't complain. I'm eating enough garlic to stay healthy."

"Good."

"Yes, sir. Garlic and olive oil will make you live forever."

I smiled. He may be right. I'll research it and let you know.

"Say, I'm looking for someone," I said. "Maybe you can help."

"Sure. I'm always willing to help a pal." He slurped some spaghetti into his mouth. "Who are you looking for?"

"A stripper named Irene Atom. She retired about fifteen years ago."

"Irene Atom? A stripper?"

"Yes. I'm told she used to work North Beach."

He stopped shoveling spaghetti into his mouth and shook his head.

"No, I'm afraid I can't help you."

"Then keep eating your garlic."

Skeets smiled and saluted me with a fork full of spaghetti.

"I'll let you know if something turns up," he said.

"I'd appreciate it."

"But I don't think anything will."

I ate a plate of first-rate pasta carbonara and then resumed my search. But it was no good. No one remembered a stripper named Irene Atom.

*　　*　　*

"You've got to find her!" Sidney screamed. "She must be around somewhere! She must be!"

"Are you sure?" I asked. "Are you certain she's still in The City?"

"She is, Winston, she is. I just know it. Even if she isn't, you must find those photos!"

I attributed Sidney's extreme paranoia to the pressure of mounting a political campaign.

"I can't find anyone who remembers her," I added.

"Winston, you've got to find her! You've got to try again. Please."

"All right, Sidney, I'll try," I sighed.

"Thank you." He relaxed slightly. "I'll reward you with a government position if you find her."

"That won't be necessary," I said. The thought of serving in government chilled me to my bones. That was not my kind of gig.

"Well, I'll find some way to reward you."

*　　*　　*

"James, any ideas on how to find Irene Atom?" As it turned

out, that was a silly question.

"Yes, sir, I do. I've been making a few inquiries on my own, and I believe I have discovered her residence."

"I say, good job!" Good chauffeur, that James. Do you know how hard? No, you probably don't.

"She is living with someone in North Beach and no longer uses the name Irene Atom."

"Not surprising. Still, it's unusual that none of the old-timers had ever heard of her. But never mind. Take me to her, James."

"Yes, sir."

James prepared the Rolls, and we were soon slicing through the late-night streets of North Beach. He drove several blocks down Columbus, then turned right onto an upwardly sloping street lined with multiple-floor apartment houses. Most of them were Victorians, but unfortunately, several modern boxes had been wedged between the older structures, and they looked like weeds growing between cracks in the sidewalk. As usual, parking was impossible. James temporarily double-parked the Rolls in front of one of the Victorians and let me out.

"She lives in Apartment Thirty-one," he said.

I nodded and approached the building. It was once white but dirt and cracked paint had turned the facade a dull tan. A man with long gray and black hair sat on the steps, and he wasn't doing anything but staring. I approached the steps, and he looked up.

"I'm looking for Irene Atom," I said.

His marble eyes were motionless. He shrugged.

"Do you live here?" I asked.

Again, he shrugged. I left him to his private world and climbed the three steps to the front door. It was a nice door consisting of dark wood with frosted glass etched with an ethereal art deco design. It could have used some refurbishing, though. I twisted the doorknob and found the door unlocked. I eased it open and stepped in. The foyer had the musty smell that foyers get after a century of sweat, tobacco smoke, and leaky windows. The mailboxes were to the right of the doorway, the stairs in front of me. Someone opened a door on the next floor, but I couldn't see who it was. I got the impression, however, that I was being watched.

I made the quick deduction that Apartment Thirty-one was on the third floor and started up the stairs. They were noisy, and I walked as softly as possible, but I still sounded like a herd of thundering Buicks. I was right about Apartment Thirty-one. It was on the third floor.

I paused at the door and heard shuffling inside. I displayed the quick thinking I am known for and decided it would be better to use a false identity and quickly thought of one. Then I knocked on the door. A scruffy, middle-aged man opened it. His hair was very short, and it stood straight up. Tiny stubbles of beard poked out of inappropriate parts of his face.

"Yeah?" he asked.

"I'd like to see Irene Atom."

"Who?"

"Irene Atom."

He looked at me funny. I thought that perhaps for once, James had gotten it wrong.

"She used to be an entertainer," I said. "Does she still live here?"

"Oh, Irene." His eyes became opaque. "What do you want to see her for?"

"I'm a journalist, and I'd like to interview her." It seemed like a good story to me.

He looked at my custom-tailored, dark gray double-breasted suit and recently shined black Italian shoes. Ferragamo, of course.

"You look like a lawyer to me," he said.

"I say, there's no need to get nasty," I said. "I truly am a journalist. From Cleveland, Ohio."

"Journalist," the man mumbled. "How do I know you're a journalist?" People in this city are so suspicious.

"You'll have to trust me, I guess."

He looked me over again. I think he liked my shoes.

"Wait a minute." He closed the door, and I heard some whispers and more shuffling. After a few minutes, he reopened the door.

"Come on in," he said.

"Thank you."

The apartment was drab. There were outlines on the walls where until recently, pictures or posters had hung. A dim table lamp balanced on a crooked end table next to a stuffed armchair leaking its stuffing. The table lamp was the only light in the room. A woman sat in the chair, and she was smothered in shadows. She rose and stepped into the musty yellow light.

"Hello, I'm Irene Atom," she said.

She must have been nearing her sixties if she hadn't already reached them. Her facial features were sharp, and her blonde hair was too young. She was attractive, not beautiful, and had the kind of face that you could stare at for hours but never fully understand.

"Hello, my name's Fred Miller," I said. Don't look that at me that way. It was the best name I could come up with at the time.

"You are?" She studied me the way a palm reader studies palms. "Then I'm glad to meet you." Her handshake was powerful. "You've met Brian." She nodded toward the man.

"Hello," I said to him.

"Fred Miller," Brian mumbled. His expression was a mass of scrambled eggs.

"So, you're a journalist?" Irene said.

"Yes, I write for *The Cleveland Times*."

"Cleveland?"

"Yes."

"What are you doing in San Francisco?"

"I'm here to write about North Beach."

"What do people in Cleveland care about North Beach?"

"Tourists care about North Beach. I write a travel column."

"Yes, of course." She wasn't impressed. "Why do you want to talk to me?"

"I'm writing a piece about how North Beach has changed over the years. I was told that you might be able to tell me about the old North Beach."

"Who told you that?"

"Some of the people I've talked to on the street."

She smiled a sinful smile.

"What would you like to know?" she asked.

"I would like to know about your past."

"My past?" Her eyelids fluttered. "It was not very exciting. It was very ordinary."

"What is ordinary for North Beach is special for Cleveland," I said.

"I suppose so." Her smile was unnerving.

"And people's lives are usually more interesting than they think."

"Are they?"

I couldn't tell whether she was buying my line or not.

"Yes. May I ask you a few questions about your life?"

Her eyes shifted to Brian and then back to me.

"If you really want to ask them," she said. "But I assure you that my life has not been very interesting." She turned and swayed back to the stuffed chair. Brian brought two metal chairs from the kitchen, and we sat down. The light from the cheap lamp cast harsh shadows on her face.

"Now, Mister, what did you say your name was?"

"Miller," I said.

"Oh, yes, Mr. Miller. How could I forget that? It's such a common name, isn't it? Now, what would you like to know?"

"Well, one of the first things people think of when they think of North Beach is Broadway and the strip joints."

"Is that what they think?"

"Well, yes." I didn't like the way the conversation had begun. "I understand you were once a stripper," I said.

She quickly looked at Brian.

"Am I wrong?" I asked.

"No, no," she fluttered. "You have it right." She crossed her legs. "You journalists have a way of getting right to the heart of the matter."

"If you don't want to talk about it, we can talk about

something else," I said, sensing her uneasiness.

"What else would people in Cleveland care to read about?" Her mouth smiled, but her eyes remained cold. She was on her guard, but she spoke with a disarming easiness.

"The old and the new?" I said. "People always like to read about how things have changed, how the good old days have gone."

"Ah, the good old days," she nodded. "In the good old days, there were real nightclubs. And real comedy clubs!" She suddenly came alive and spoke with infectious enthusiasm. "But sadly, they are gone. I think the good old days ended when 'The Green Apple' closed, don't you?"

"Yes," I nodded. "That certainly left a void."

Heat rose from her eyes.

"Would you happen to have any old photographs?" I asked.

She looked at Brian, then back at me. I thought she was going to say no.

"I don't mean X-rated," I said.

"What do you mean?" she inquired. She almost spoke with a Southern accent.

"Oh, something innocent. Suitable for the newspapers."

"Suitable for the newspapers!" she laughed.

"For Cleveland newspapers," I said. "Pictures that would show how things were in the old North Beach, you know, so that

I could do a before-and-after."

"Well, I may have something." She motioned to Brian. He left the room and returned with a box. Irene opened it and shuffled through some pictures. I recognized a young Sidney in several of them and tried to contain my excitement, but I'm sure my eyes widened a wee bit. The photos didn't look very incriminating to me, just Sidney and Irene holding each other and smiling at the camera. I perused the photos.

"Yes, these are very good," I said. "Just what the people in Cleveland would like to see."

"Are they?"

"Yes. Would you be interested in selling them?" I knew Sidney would put up the cash.

"All of them?"

"As many as you would like to sell." She would get suspicious if I was only interested in the photos with Sidney in them. At times I can be very clever, don't you think?

She looked at me. Her eyes had cooled.

"I'm afraid not," she said. She took the photos back, placed them in the box, and handed it to Brian. I watched him intently as he took them back to the other room.

"I can pay you a good price," I said.

"It's not the money," she said. "They have sentimental value. These photos are all that remain of my life. I can't possibly part with them."

"Do you have the negatives? Perhaps I could make copies."

"No, there are no negatives. All I have are those photos. They are the only remnants of my good old days."

"I see. Well, think about my offer, would you?"

"I won't change my mind."

"If you do, leave a message for me at the Kensington Park Hotel."

She smiled and rose from her chair.

"Now, I'm afraid I must go, Mr. Miller," she said. "Brian and I help a friend clean up his restaurant every night. He closes at midnight."

I looked at my watch. It was ten minutes to twelve.

"I'm sorry I've taken so much of your time," I said. "I do appreciate your cooperation."

"It's been my pleasure." Her handshake was sly.

"Please think about those photos," I said. "I'd settle for even just a few of them."

"Perhaps I could spare one," she said. "I'll think about it. No promises, though."

"Fair enough," I said.

Brian led me to the door and closed it behind me. I walked down the stairs and out of the building. Even as I climbed into the Rolls, I felt as if I was being watched.

"Does she have the pictures?" James asked.

"Yes," I said. "I offered to buy them, but she wouldn't sell."

"Pity, sir."

*   *   *

"She won't sell them?" Sidney screamed. He was unhappy.

"No."

"Winston, I've got to have those photos!" he yelled. His voice sounded like an Austin Healy 3000 on five cylinders. You do you know what an Austin Healy 3000 on five cylinders sounds like, don't you? If you don't, it's damned unpleasant.

"If she doesn't sell them, you'll have to get them some other way," Sidney continued. "Money is no obstacle."

"I'll do my best."

There was a pause.

"I'm sorry, Winston. I know you will, and I didn't mean to suggest you wouldn't. It's just that you know how important this election is to me."

"Yes, I'm beginning to."

"Good. I knew I could count on you."

"I don't have them yet."

"But you will get them. I know you will. Good job."

*　　　*　　　*

It was a crowded North Beach Saturday night. The neon lights buzzed with electric excitement, and the magical aroma of garlic and olive oil carried on the sea breeze. James parked the Rolls near Irene's building.

"They should be gone by now," I said. It was a few minutes before midnight. "If you have any trouble finding the box, go to the window. I can see it from here."

"Yes, sir."

"Otherwise, I'll just wait for you. Good luck."

"Thank you, sir."

James left the Rolls and walked down the sidewalk. I rolled down the window and rested my arm on the sill. I'm not a chauffeur, so I'm allowed to do that. Seconds later, two familiar-looking men passed by carrying suitcases. One of them wore sunglasses even though it was night, and he had short hair that stood straight up. The other man kept his head down, but I was sure I had seen him somewhere before. It bugged me.

"Good night, Mr. Churchill," one of them said to me as they passed.

His words hit me like a left hook to the body. How did he know my name? By the time I had recovered from the shock and went after them they were gone. North Beach had engulfed them.

I ran back to the Rolls and found James leaning out of the window of Irene's apartment. Something was wrong. The long-haired man was no longer on the steps. He had probably located a new home, steps with running water, or a better view. I dashed into the apartment building. The lobby was quiet. Much too quiet. I was no longer being watched.

I jumped up the stairs with all the getup of a steeple chase horse and dashed into Apartment Thirty-one. An unshaded light bulb lit the apartment and filled the space with film noir shadows. I know a vacant apartment when I see one, and this was a vacant apartment.

"James, what's going on?"

"This was on the chair," he said.

"What is it?" I took a large envelope from him.

"It has your name on it, sir."

"What?" My stomach churned like a bubbling fondue. "I used an alias with her. How did she know my real name?" I ripped open the envelope and took out a letter. It read:

My Dear Mr. Winston Churchill,

I know who you are, and I know that Sidney sent you. I had been warned that if he ever wanted to get those photographs back, he would surely ask someone like you to do it. I did well to heed those warnings, for you were very good. It was not until I tricked you into revealing your true knowledge of the old North Beach that I was certain it was you. Who in Cleveland would have known about "The Green Apple"?

I realize that you probably do not know the real significance of those pictures. If you did, I am sure you would never have agreed to obtain them for Sidney. He probably told you that I would use them to blackmail him. Let me tell you the true story.

I do not know how well you know Sidney. Socially, he appears to be an angel. Privately he can be a real bastard. I am not going to go into all the sordid details, but suffice it to say that he is not above inflicting bodily harm. We had a very turbulent relationship those many years ago, and although it is now over, I still do not trust him.

So, you see, I must keep those photographs. They are my only form of protection against this man who can be such a monster. Rest assured that I will not use them to blackmail him. I have no vendetta, and as long as he stays away from me, I will cause him no harm. I am leaving the country with Brian and hope that the distance will protect me from any further intrusion caused by Sidney Felstein. I am leaving him a poster from my entertaining days which he might care to possess, and I remain, dear Winston Churchill,

Very truly yours,
Irene Atom

"Ha!" My fingers were numb.

"Sir?"

I handed James the letter, unfolded the poster, and received a second shock. The poster was from Finocchio's. Above a picture of a young Irene Atom were the words: Irene Atom, Female Impersonator.

"It's her!" I yelled.

"We've been had, sir."

"Indeed, we have." I looked at the poster again. I was a bit miffed, yet I couldn't help but admire how Irene had outsmarted me.

"What a clever woman," I said. "What a clever, clever woman." I couldn't keep the grin from my face.

I rolled up the poster.

"James, I think I shall keep this poster for myself."

"Very good, sir."

I went to the open window and stared at the North Beach streets that had helped Irene Atom elude my grasp. The cool bay air slapped my face.

"Good night, Irene!" I said.

8 THE ROGUE MAKES A COMEBACK

The thrill of having been so cleverly outwitted by Irene Atom was temporary, and I soon fell into a despondency that not even my Rolls Royce could cure. Do you have any idea of how despondent that is? No, you probably don't. Well, let me tell you, it's very despondent. To top it off, I had no place to stay and was forced to check back into the Kensington Park Hotel.

*   *   *

The doorman said "good morning" with a New York accent as he opened the brass-rimmed doors. It was a clear, winter San Francisco morning and a sharp, ocean-tinged breeze slapped my face. What a way to start the day.

I pulled my dark green, almost brown, Canali overcoat tight and walked into the wind. There's nothing like a good overcoat to keep the chill from one's bones. My overcoat had been meticulously crafted from the finest Merino wool by the hands of the finest Italian tailors. Speaking of Merino wool, do you know that each Merino sheep produces up to ten kilograms of wool? Perhaps you don't. If not, you probably also do not know that Merino sheep were originally from the Mediterranean basin and were taken to Australia and New Zealand in the 18th Century. If you do know that, then consider yourself one of an impressively knowledgeable minority. But I digress…

I found a corner newsstand on Post Street and bought the day's edition of the *San Francisco Chronicle*. Yes, I could have purchased the paper from a more convenient outlet, but the continued existence of small corner newsstands in the modern world is remote, and I wanted to do my part in delaying their demise. Perhaps you have noticed my tendency to support the underdog.

As I passed the Ritz Deli, I noticed Sarah Everton having an intimate cup of coffee with a man I think I may have met before. She saw me through the tall windows and motioned for me to join her.

"Good morning, Sarah," I said.

"Good morning, Winston." She grabbed my hands and kissed me a bit too dramatically. "It's so nice to see you. It's been such a long time."

Her smile restored the youth to the outer reaches of her face. It had been a while since I had seen her, and I was surprised to see that she was becoming as portly as her husband. Have you noticed how wealth has a way of ravaging the body? Perhaps you have.

The man rose.

"Do you know Tom Sledgeton?" Sarah asked, presenting her breakfast partner. He was a tall man, also well on his way to becoming portly. He wore an expensive suit that he had bought off the rack without alteration. It's a crime to pay that much money and not get bespoke or at least made-to-measure. Style, you either have it, or you don't, and if you have it, well, enough said about that. Trust me, Mr. Sledgeton did not have it.

"We may have met before," I said to him. "I'm Winston Churchill."

"How do you do?" he said. He looked me over the way an investor looks over stock quotations.

"Tom's a good friend of Rodney's," Sarah explained.

"And how is Rodney?" I asked.

"Fine. He's out of town on business. He'll be back this afternoon. We're having a dinner party Friday night. My horoscope said it would be a good night for a party. Why don't you join us?"

"I'd love to."

"Good," she said. "Parties are always better when you're around. Something exciting always seems to happen."

"I'm sure she meant that in a positive way," Sledgeton said.

"Of course, I did!" Sarah laughed.

"Thank you," I said.

"Well, it's been nice meeting you," Tom Sledgeton said, suddenly grabbing my hand.

I took the hint.

"Yes, goodbye," I said. I kissed Sarah on the cheek and left the deli with renewed vigor. The prospect of an elegant dinner party brightened my spirits. Just so you know, I'll tell you a bit of my dinner party hosts.

The Everton's were young money on a buying binge they hoped would secure their place in established society. They lived in a small palace, imaginatively called "Everton House", on Broadway, west of Van Ness. Pretty ritzy territory. My Rolls Royce always looked good in their driveway.

I had known Sarah's husband, Rodney, for quite some time. He was an impetuous man, relentless in his pursuit of success. His business was prosperous, his shotgun collection impressive, his parties expensive. Friday evening promised to be eventful, if nothing else.

*　　*　　*

James easily conquered the Friday night traffic, and we arrived promptly at Everton House. It had been raining on and off, so I had layered a genuine Burberry trench coat over my brown, heavy wool bespoke suit from Henry Poole. Sarah's butler answered the door. It slipped from his grasp as he opened it and banged against the wall. Very shabby. Not something a proper butler would have done. Then again, he didn't look much like a proper butler. He was in his mid-twenties with a sculpted physique that should have been adorning a piazza in Rome. He was undoubtedly Sarah's type.

"Winston Churchill," I announced to him.

"Who?"

"Winston Churchill."

I handed him my trench coat. He reluctantly took it. I'm sure my sartorial flair was wasted on him. He didn't look like the kind of man who could tell the difference between a real Burberry trench coat and a cheap imitation. In case you don't know, the secret to a real Burberry is in the cotton. It is chemically treated while still in the yarn, woven tightly into cloth, and proofed again before being made into a garment. Class will always tell, won't it?

The butler looked at James.

"Where shall we put your driver?"

"He's not my driver; he's my chauffeur."

"Oh, then he'd better come inside."

The butler led us into a large living room decorated with dark blue and maroon furniture. The furniture was fashion magazine chic and appeared to be permanently fastened to the floor. A stone mantle imported from France sat above the fireplace, and a fire crackled in the hearth. The random mixing of interior design styles and eras did not appeal to my decorating tastes.

Rodney, shotgun in hand, stood in the center of the living room. Two men, one of them Tom Sledgeton, stood in jealous trances before him. Rodney saw me enter and smiled.

"Winston!" he called. "It's good to see you again. Sarah told me she had invited you. I'm glad you could come."

I joined the trio and shook a massive hand attached to the log-shaped arm that protruded from Rodney's canyon-width shoulder. Yes, everything about Rodney was big.

"I'd never miss one of your parties," I said to him. "You're looking good. And I say, so is that shotgun."

Rodney beamed.

"Yes, I just bought it at an auction. I outbid these two for it."

Sledgeton and the other man snarled.

"Oh, by the way, do you know these fine gentlemen?" Rodney asked, exaggerating his pronunciation of "gentlemen."

"Tom Sledgeton," Sledgeton immediately said to me as if we had never met.

"I'm Edgar Littleton," the other said as he shook my hand. He was a small man with Ivy League glasses and a bald head.

"Pleased to meet you," I said.

"We went to Wharton Business School together," Rodney said. "We've been friends ever since. We have the same hobbies, the same interests, the same everything. Why we could be triplets!" he laughed. "They're a bit sore at me now because I outbid them for this shotgun. She's a beauty, isn't she?"

Rodney raised the double-barrel shotgun for all to see. It had a gold pheasant intricately engraved above the trigger, and the stock glowed like finely polished furniture. It was the most beautiful shotgun I had ever seen. It was even more beautiful than the guns Ted Nance collected.

"It's a vintage A. J. Roberts," Rodney said. "Cost me $125,000."

I whistled.

"But she's worth every penny," Rodney continued. "Look at that detail work. And the barrel has not been re-blued. That shine is original."

"You've got yourself a masterpiece," I said.

"I know. And they don't." Rodney poked his nose at his friends and grinned. "Edgar went out of the bidding surprisingly early. But Tom fought me all the way."

"Until you drastically overpaid for it," Tom said. "Still, I should have continued bidding. That A. J. Roberts would have been the crown jewel of my collection. I wanted it badly, but Rodney always seems to know my limits."

Rodney laughed and patted Sledgeton on the shoulder.

"Go get a drink and drown your sorrow," he said.

Sledgeton nodded and slithered off.

"I've got a new company, too, Winston."

Edgar frowned and adjusted his eyeglass frames.

"Edgar tried to outbid me for it," Rodney chuckled. "But he lost his nerve. He always does."

"That isn't so," Edgar growled.

"Oh, Edgar, why don't you go have a drink with Tom. You can drink away your losses together."

"Honestly, Rodney," Edgar said. "One of these days, you're going to pay for your arrogance."

"Ha! You guys couldn't afford to make me pay," Rodney laughed.

Edgar shook his head and stormed off. Rodney laughed until he ran out of laughs and turned to me.

"Winston, the best thing in life is winning," he said. "Like winning that shotgun from Tom and winning that company from Edgar. Winning is truly everything. It's the food we eat and the air we breathe. Yes, winning is what it's all about. Winning makes life worth living."

"What about how you play the game?" I asked.

"If you play the game right, you win."

"Whatever makes you happy."

"Winning makes me happy, Winston. And my shotguns."

"Are you still talking about that shotgun?" a woman asked.

"Of course," Rodney smiled.

The woman joined us and was swallowed into Rodney's friendly embrace. She looked a bit frail, but her face was lively. Her eyes were like marbles, and they rolled underneath a pair of artificially enhanced eyelids.

"Winston, this is Edgar's wife, Agnes."

"Hello," I said to her. "I'm Winston Churchill."

"My, Rodney, you have such important friends," she giggled.

"I do my best," Rodney laughed.

"Have you met my husband?" Agnes asked me.

"Yes," I said. "And Tom Sledgeton."

"The whole crew!" she shook her head and chuckled.

"Excuse me," Rodney said to me. "I'm going to put this gun away. Agnes will keep you company."

Agnes nodded and smiled.

"He's been showing everyone that darn shotgun," she said. "I'm tired of hearing about it. He's just rubbing it in, though, trying to make the other two feel bad. They've been competing against each other like that ever since college. I've never seen anything like it. Once one of them wants something, the others also have to have it. It drives me crazy. But they seem to enjoy it. I guess it's just one of those things women don't understand."

"Your husband didn't seem to enjoy losing that company," I said.

"Oh, he'll get over it. He always does. I don't know how they've managed to stay friends all these years."

"Rodney, put that gun away," Sarah yelled from across the room.

"All right, all right," Rodney said. "Hey, Winston, come over here."

I smiled at Agnes.

"Sorry, but I'm wanted," I said.

"That's all right. One should never keep Rodney waiting."

I joined Rodney in front of a large gun case in the far corner of the room.

"Look at this one," he said, taking another shotgun from the case. "It's a Parker."

"Very nice." It looked like one of Ted Nance's guns.

"I think you've seen the rest of them."

I scanned the case.

"Yes, I think so," I said.

He closed the case and locked it.

"Here, hang on to this for me, will you?" he said. He handed me a small, tan envelope. "Keep it with the others."

"Sure."

*   *   *

Have you ever noticed how elegant dinner parties raise one's spirits? If you inhabit my milieu, you have; if you don't, you probably haven't. But it's true. Trust me. The Everton's party had worked its magic and cured my malaise. The Rolls had regained its charm, and I felt good enough to order a new suit. I will not disclose the name of my tailor, but I will tell you that the suit will be double-breasted and cut from a dark gray birds-eye fabric that you may have seen on Humphrey Bogart. And, of course, I had to acquire accessories to match: a tie, pocket square, and belt. When one owns a Rolls Royce, one's wardrobe must measure up. We'll talk about shoes later.

I was in the best of spirits when Monday dawned. The hotel delivered the morning *Chronicle* to my room with my breakfast. I was a little disappointed that I wouldn't have to purchase it from the corner newsstand. I sat back in a comfortable chair next to my room's window and took a sprinkling of news with my orange juice. All very civilized. All very civilized until the bottom half of the front page. A two-column story shattered my morning: Rodney Everton was missing!

According to an exclusive *Chronicle* story, Rodney had not returned from a Saturday hunting trip. Sarah Everton had expected him home that afternoon, but he never returned. She was a bit miffed at the police for telling her that Rodney had not been missing long enough to warrant a full investigation. As the British would say, it was all a bit rum.

Under the circumstances, the civilized thing to do was to visit Sarah and offer her my services. I called for the Rolls, and James immediately took me to Everton House. Sarah answered the door herself.

"The butler had to take a short leave of absence," she apologized. He had probably banged the door once too often. Even Sarah has her limits.

"What about Rodney?" I asked.

"Oh, Winston, it's terrible." She clung to her damp handkerchief the way a wet leaf clings to a car's windshield. She led me into the study.

"Tell me what happened."

"Friday night after the party, Rodney told me that he was going hunting in the morning. He got up around five o'clock, and I made him coffee, and then he took his new shotgun and left. He said he would be home late in the afternoon, but that was the last time I saw him."

I walked over to the gun case. The A. J. Roberts was missing.

Curious.

"I'm sure there's been a dreadful accident," she continued. "It's the only explanation."

"Don't jump to conclusions," I said. "He hasn't been gone very long, and he may have decided to stay longer. Perhaps the hunting was good."

"Oh, Winston, you sound just like the police! Rodney would have called me if he was going to stay longer. He always does. It's not like him just to stay away."

"Did he go with anyone?" I asked.

"I don't know. He didn't say. He often goes with Tom or Edgar. Tom did not go. I don't know about Edgar."

"Have you talked to Edgar?"

"No. Maybe the police have. I don't know. Oh, Winston, I'm so worried." Her eyes darkened for a second.

"I'll do what I can to help if you'd like," I said.

"Oh, Winston, I appreciate that, but Tom is taking care of things."

Tom Sledgeton entered the room on cue. He was surprised to see me.

"I came over when I read the news," I said to him.

He nodded. Sarah went to him.

"Tom's been so good during all of this," she said. "I don't know what I would do without him."

"She exaggerates my value," Sledgeton said. "But it's important to help friends in need."

"Yes, very important," I agreed.

"Thanks for your concern," Sledgeton said, leading me to the door. "But I think everything is under control for the moment."

"Yes, I'll be all right," Sarah said. "I'm eternally grateful for your visit."

I nodded and left Everton House.

"Any news, sir?" James asked.

"Rodney went hunting and never returned." I paused for dramatic effect. "And the A. J. Roberts is missing. According to Sarah, he took it hunting."

"Then there has been foul play, sir."

"Indeed, there has, James, indeed there has."

*   *   *

The following day I was stirred from a restful slumber by a raging telephone. Agnes Littleton was on the line.

"Winston, I'm sorry to bother you, not knowing you all that well and whatnot, but I don't know who to turn to. You've heard about Rodney Everton's disappearance?"

"Yes."

"Well, the police have just been talking to Edgar. You don't think they think he may have something to do with it, do you?"

"Probably just routine," I said.

"I hope you're right, but they seem to believe that he went hunting with Rodney on Saturday morning. But he didn't. I don't like this, Winston. The police are asking terrible questions. What should I do?"

"Don't worry. If Edgar is innocent, he has nothing to worry about."

"Of course, he's innocent!" She yelped like a yelping terrier.

"Then just sit tight. I'll take care of things."

"Thank you so much, Winston. May I call you Winston?"

"Certainly."

"Then thank you again, Winston."

I hung up, and the phone immediately rang again. It was Sarah.

"Winston, they found Rodney's truck in the Sierras! But there's no sign of Rodney. Oh, Winston, I'm afraid he's dead!"

"Calm down, Sarah. Why would you think that?"

"I don't know. Sometimes, I can be kind of psychic. I'm sorry to bother you, Winston. I'm just so worried."

"I understand. Have they found anything to indicate Rodney has been injured?"

"I don't know. They didn't tell me much, but I don't think they did."

"Well, don't give up hope, Sarah."

"I won't."

"Is there anything I can do?"

"No. Tom's still taking care of me. I just thought you'd want to know about the truck."

"Yes, I'm glad you called. Please let me know if anything else comes up."

"I will."

I hung up the phone and went back to bed. My head had just hit the pillow when the pounding on my door started.

"Strike three, I'm up," I growled.

The pounding wouldn't stop, so I opened the door. A man in dirty clothes and a muddy face barged in and tracked mud across the floor.

"Winston," he said.

I was surprised to hear my name and a little alarmed at his presence in my room. He reminded me of some creature from a low-budget horror movie.

"Winston, it's me."

I looked at him more closely. It took some imagination, but I eventually recognized the face before me. It was Rodney Everton!

"Rodney," I said. "You're missing."

"I am?"

"Yes. What happened to you?"

"I don't know," he shook his head.

"Sit down. Can I get you something to drink?"

He sat down and scratched his head. Tiny flakes of mud and leaves fell onto his shoulder.

"I'll take whiskey if you have it."

I found a small bottle of Jim Beam in the minibar.

"Rocks?" I asked.

"Straight."

I poured the whiskey into a glass and handed it to him.

"Now tell me what happened," I asked.

"I honestly don't know. I can't seem to remember very much."

"What do you remember?"

"I remember the party. And I remember waking up in the wilderness. But I don't recall anything in between. I must have been drugged and dumped somewhere. Winston, what's going on?"

"You've been reported missing," I said. "There was a nice piece about you in the *Chronicle*."

"There was?"

"Yes."

I handed him the paper. He read the story and seemed pleased with the attention it was bringing him.

"So, how long have I been gone?"

"A couple of days."

His eyes blinked a few times.

"That explains why I'm so hungry. Say, what day is it anyway?"

"Monday."

"Monday!" His eyelids jumped, and a few more mud flakes fell from them like snowflakes.

"Yes. By the way, how did you get here?"

"I wandered through the woods for a long time, then early this morning, I found my way into some small town. I jumped in the back of a truck bound for San Francisco. I suspected foul play, so I came straight to you."

"Then you haven't been home?"

"No. I thought it might be easier to get to the bottom of this if no one knew I was back."

"Good thinking," I said. Rodney hadn't gotten rich by being dumb.

"How's Sarah?" he asked.

"Concerned. But Tom Sledgeton has been providing comfort."

"Has he?" He rubbed his jaw with a dirty thumb and index finger.

"Yes," I said.

He finished the Jim Beam and attempted to sort things out.

"So, what's the story?" he said. "How did I disappear?"

"According to Sarah, Friday night, you told her you were going hunting in the morning. You left early, and that was it. They found your truck in the Sierras, but they didn't find you. Sarah thinks you may have had a hunting accident."

"This was no accident. I don't know what happened, I'm still groggy, but this was no accident. Winston, we have to find out who did this to me."

"Edgar Littleton, perhaps?" I said.

"Edgar? Why Edgar? Why would he do something like this?"

"He is a hunting partner of yours, isn't he?"

"Yes."

"And you did outbid him for that company, didn't you?"

"Yes, I did." Rodney paused and then smiled. "And don't forget, I also beat Tom out of that shotgun."

"Yes, and it's missing."

"What? My A. J. Roberts is missing?"

"Yes, you allegedly took it hunting with you. Curious, isn't it?"

"It's more than curious; it's dastardly. Who could have done such a thing?"

"I say we find out."

"How?" Rodney asked.

"We'll set a few traps and see what we catch."

Rodney smiled. A true sportsman always enjoys a good hunt.

*   *   *

James had once again used Connally hide food on the Rolls' leather upholstery, and the seats smelled intoxicating. The rich aroma cuddled me as I sat down.

"Good job, James."

"Thank you, sir." He tilted his head and waited for instructions.

"To Everton House."

"Yes, sir."

Everton House was quiet. Tom Sledgeton's Mercedes occupied the driveway. It's nice to have a car like that to park next to because it makes the Rolls look much better.

Sarah again answered the door herself.

"The butler's still away?" I asked.

"I'm afraid so." Embarrassment crossed her face as if she had turned it on with a switch. She led me into the study. Sledgeton was stuffed into a gothic chair with *The Wall Street Journal* glued to his hands, and he did not rise when we entered the room. Poor manners if you ask me.

"Any more news?" I asked.

"No," Sarah shook her head. "All they've found so far is his truck. There's been no trace of Rodney at all."

"Have they found his shotgun?"

"No."

"What are the police doing now?" I asked.

"Waiting," Sledgeton said. He didn't take his eyes off the paper.

"Waiting?" I grumbled. "Is that all?"

"Yes, Winston," Sarah said. She looked me in the eyes and gave me her best Mary Astor look. "I don't think they're doing enough."

"What more can they do?" Sledegton said. "The Sierra's a big place, and I'm sure they don't have enough men to search everywhere."

"I suppose you're right," Sarah said. "But I wish they could do more. I wish there were something I could do to help."

"Perhaps there is," I said.

"What do you mean?" Sarah asked. The surprise in her eyes was genuine.

"Have you thought about consulting a psychic?" I asked.

"What?"

"A psychic. They have been known to help the police solve mysteries and find missing people."

"You can't be serious," Sledgeton said. He lowered his paper and glared at me the way a dog owner glares at a new puppy who has just done his business on the living room carpet.

"I am serious," I said. "It's worth considering."

Sledgeton shook his head and turned his attention back to the

Journal. Sarah turned pensive. She was very good at that.

"But a psychic?" she said. "How unusual."

"Rodney's disappearance is unusual, don't you agree? Sometimes you must be creative in these matters and try untraditional approaches."

She thought for a moment.

"Maybe you're right," she said. "You are experienced in these matters."

"Sarah!" Sledgeton tossed the Journal and went to her. "Don't be silly."

"I'm not being silly. Winston may be on to something. I've read about these psychics. They have helped the police find people and solve mysteries. I'm a believer. Besides, I've got to do something, Tom. I can't rely solely on the police. They aren't getting anywhere. Do you have any better ideas?"

"No, I don't have any ideas at all," Sledgeton said. "But I think Winston's idea is ridiculous. Really, Sarah. You read too many horoscopes."

"Don't belong to the Flat Earth Society, do you?" I asked him.

"What?" My sarcasm was wasted on him, and not surprising given his poor taste in clothes.

"Then it's settled," Sarah said. "Where can I find a psychic?"

"I know someone who may be able to help," I said.

"Yes, I thought you might," Sledgeton howled.

"How do we go about this?" Sarah asked.

"Sarah! I can't believe you're serious about this." Sledgeton stormed out of the room, shaking his head so wildly that I thought it would twist off his shoulders. It didn't.

"Leave it to me," I said. "I'll bring the psychic here. I think Tom, Edgar, and Agnes should be present."

"Will there be a séance?" she asked.

"Yes, but not one like you've ever seen before," I said.

*　　　*　　　*

"I think this is outrageous," Sledgeton whispered to me.

"You don't believe in the supernatural?"

"No. I don't think you do, either. I think you're taking advantage of Sarah."

"Why would I do that?"

My question stumped him. He was about to continue his attack but froze when Madame Faux, the Seer of All Things, entered the room. She looked half gypsy and half renaissance minstrel.

"I am ready to begin," she announced.

"Shall we all sit around a table and hold hands?" Sarah asked.

Madame Faux threw her a disgusted look.

"We don't do things that way anymore," she said. "This isn't

TV."

"Oh," Sarah blushed.

"But we will need a room where we can all sit closely," Madam Faux said.

"The study?" I suggested.

"Yes," Sarah said. "The study will be fine."

Madame Faux and I arranged several chairs and a sofa into a semicircle that faced the door. I placed a small table in front of the chairs, and Madame Faux balanced a candle on the table.

"We shall begin," she announced. "Everyone, please sit down."

I lit the candle and turned out the lights. The room was very dark, and the candle cast creepy shadows on the walls and the large bookcase behind the circle of chairs. It was a perfect setup. Madame Faux sat behind the table and faced us.

"My, it's dark in here," Agnes said.

"It is supposed to be," Madame Faux said. "We are dealing with psychic forces."

Sledgeton giggled.

"Good, a disbeliever," Madame Faux said. "It is always better to have at least one." She slowly closed her eyes. "All I require is your silence."

"You shall have it," Sledgeton yawned. He leaned back on the sofa and closed his eyes. However, he quickly awoke when

Madame Faux began chanting in some foreign language that sounded like Latin played backward. She certainly knew how to captivate an audience. Then she stopped chanting and went into a trance.

"Edgar Littleton," she said from her trance. Her voice had become deeper, and it sounded as if it was echoing off the walls of the Grand Canyon. How did she do that?

Edgar let out a little yelp at the mention of his name. The poor lad seemed a bit shaky.

"Tom Sledgeton," Madame Faux's voice boomed deeper off the canyon walls.

"Yeah?"

"I sense a connection between you and Rodney. A strong connection. An undying friendship."

"Everyone knows that," Sledgeton snarled.

"Shhh," Sarah whispered.

Sledgeton shrugged.

"But the tie that binds you is now broken," Madame Faux continued. "The friendship of many years has been severed."

"What is she talking about?" Edgar whispered.

"I sense hostility," Madame Faux said. "Hostility and a sense of great sadness. I sense the spirit of Rodney Everton."

Agnes gasped.

"The spirit is approaching," Madame Faux continued. "It is a tortured soul, one betrayed by friendship. So sad, so sad."

"She's giving me the creeps," Sarah said.

Sledgeton rose.

"I'm going to put a stop to this right now," he said.

The haunting voice that appeared to be coming from every corner of the room halted him.

"Where's my shotgun?" the voice asked.

Sledgeton froze.

"Rodney," Sarah whispered, looking like she had seen a ghost. "Oh my god, it's Rodney!"

"That damn shotgun," Agnes said. "That's all he ever thought about."

"Which one of you has my shotgun?" the voice continued.

"It can't be Rodney," Sarah said. "It can't be."

"Why not?" I asked. She didn't answer.

"This is some kind of hoax," Sledgeton said.

"Do you have my shotgun, Tom?"

Sledgeton stiffened.

"Still think it's a hoax?" Agnes asked him.

"Sarah, do you have my shotgun?"

Sarah recoiled. Suddenly Agnes screamed. A shadowy shape flickered near the doorway.

"It's Rodney's ghost!" Agnes screamed.

Sledgeton squinted.

"That's no ghost," he said. "It's casting a shadow." He started toward the doorway.

"Where's my shotgun?" Rodney yelled, much louder than before. "Where's my shotgun?"

"Shut up, Rodney," Sarah screamed. "Shut up!"

"Where's my shotgun?" Rodney continued.

Someone blew out the candle, and there was movement in the darkness. I heard noises from behind the bookcase, and when the lights came on, Sarah had the A. J. Roberts pointed at Rodney.

"Go back to hell, Rodney," Sarah screamed.

She pulled the trigger, but the gun did not fire. She pulled the trigger again. Then again.

"It won't shoot without this," I said, tossing the tan envelope Rodney had given me at the dinner party onto the table.

"What's that?" Sledgeton asked.

"The firing pin," Rodney said. "I remove the firing pin from all of my guns and give them to Winston for safekeeping. It makes the guns safer to store in the house and also makes them useless if they're stolen."

James appeared and took the A. J. Roberts from Sarah.

"Then you're not dead," Sledgeton said to Rodney.

Rodney stepped forward.

"Does this feel like a dead man?" he asked. He reared back and landed a left jab to Sledgeton's stomach.

Sledgeton coughed and grunted and fell backward. He stumbled over a chair and fell to the floor. Sarah went to his aid. She looked up at me.

"How did you know it was me?" she asked.

"I didn't," I said. "I thought it was Tom."

Sledgeton tried to pick himself off the floor, his chest heaving from his deep breaths.

"Me?" he wheezed.

"Yes. I knew Rodney's disappearance had something to do with that shotgun. A true collector would never hunt with a valuable gun like that A. J. Roberts. The risk of damaging it is too great. Then there was the matter of the firing pin. I knew how badly you wanted that shotgun, so I penciled you in as the prime suspect. Of course, when I learned of your affair with Sarah, I became fairly certain that she was an accomplice."

Sledgeton turned to Sarah.

"Then you took the gun," he said to her.

"Yes. But I did it for you. I knew how much you wanted it, so I decided to get it for you. I paid the butler to kill Rodney. I drugged Rodney's coffee Saturday morning, then the butler took him away. He was supposed to make it look like a hunting accident. It seems as if the useless clown screwed it up.

"Anyway, I was sick of Rodney. I wanted to be with you, Tom. I wanted to be free of Rodney once and for all. I wanted him to be a loser for a change, and I wanted to make you a winner. I wanted to make you happy. I knew that gun would make you happy. You see, I did it all for you."

Sledgeton was moved. He kissed Sarah and held her close. Rodney glared at them. Fortunately, the shotgun was still inoperable.

"Why did you go along with this stupid séance?" Sledgeton asked her.

"I had to appear to be doing something to find Rodney. If I hadn't, Winston would have become suspicious, and he would have uncovered the whole thing. A séance seemed harmless enough."

"But he uncovered it anyway," Agnes said.

"Yes, he did," Rodney said. "He uncovered a few other things as well." His laser-beam eyes tore into Sledgeton.

"You leave him alone," Sarah said.

"I'll do with him as I please."

"Oh, yeah?" Sledgeton said. "That's tough talk from someone who's supposed to be a ghost."

"I'll turn you into a real ghost," Rodney yelled.

I took Madame Faux by the arm.

"Come on," I said. "Let's go. This conversation is becoming much too spirited. Home, James."

9 CHOCOLATE COVERED ROGUE

Have you ever been to a chocolate tasting? That's right, a chocolate tasting. Don't worry if you haven't. I had never been to one before receiving a hand-delivered invitation from Pierre Lupo. The invitation arrived on paper so thick you could have built a house with it. The elegant tan envelope was hand-addressed in maroon ink and contained a tiny piece of chocolate wrapped in gold foil; a nice touch that told me Pierre had hired the best help in The City to throw his party. Very impressive, very expensive, very Pierre.

I suppose you should know a few things about Pierre. Pierre Lupo was an importer of snooty gourmet foods, and he also fancied himself to be somewhat of a gourmet chef. The verdict was still out on the latter. He was a passionate man, and his invitation surely meant chocolate was his latest passion.

I unwrapped the small piece of chocolate and contemplated

the sticky sartorial dilemma before me: what does one wear to a chocolate tasting? If you know me, you know I always dress for the occasion. Black tie and tails were too formal; tweeds and plus-fours too casual. Perhaps one of Savile Row's more modern cuts or one of those expertly tailored suits from Naples - Italy, not Florida. I settled on Naples.

Such an occasion also required appropriate footwear. I'm sure I've told you before that purchasing of shoes should never be taken lightly. Lobb's in Paris has specific rules a gentleman should follow. These rules begin with the three levels of broguing: formal, town, and sportive — the more decorative the broguing, the more casual the shoe.

In the end, my choice was untraditional: a fine pair of loafers with leather so soft you could sleep in them. Well, chocolate tasting is a rather adventurous event where even the most casual Oxford or Darby would be out of place. You'd understand if you had ever been to one.

*　　*　　*

I was staying, uninvited, in a temporarily vacant, one-hundred-year-old, three-bedroom house on Greenwich Street in The City's Telegraph Hill neighborhood. I admired the view of Coit Tower as I dressed for the party. James readied the Rolls and had it waiting in front of the house before I had finished dressing. I exited the house. He opened the rear door, and I slid into the sumptuous back seat. The door closed with a comforting thud. He cautiously maneuvered the Rolls through San Francisco's Financial District to Pierre's Washington Street condo. In case you don't know, Washington Street is a trendy avenue near the Bay within walking distance of San Francisco's financial district.

Pierre's condo was in a nouveau turn-of-the-century red brick building that slumbered over a two-block area like a sprawled lion. Vibrant pink flowers sprouted from green planters that sprouted from red windowsills. Quite elegant, even though everything did look a bit too planned and a bit too perfect.

Parking, however, was far from perfect. It was impossible, as usual, and James had to deposit me at the curb.

"Join me when you find an appropriate place to park the Rolls," I said.

"Yes, sir."

He drove off, and I admired the Silver Cloud III as it effortlessly sailed down the street. What a magnificent automobile! But I digress.

I adjusted my tie, a nice Armani piece (well, I did say chocolate tasting was an adventurous event) and searched for Pierre's home. One couldn't miss it. Brown plaques with red arrows directed guests to the tasting, and they did not lead me astray. An attractive young woman stood guard outside his condo and allowed me to enter only after checking my invitation.

"Enjoy the tasting, Mr. Churchill." She smiled at me with the kind of smile you find on the front cover of glossy fashion magazines.

"Thank you," I said. I winked at her and entered the condo.

Pierre immediately greeted me.

"Winston, so nice to see you," he said. His beefy body betrayed his obsessive love of food, and his rotund and puffy face was a small replica of his torso.

"Thanks for inviting me," I said.

"It wouldn't be the same without you."

"Am I to deduce from this chocolate tasting that your new interest in life is chocolate?" I said.

"Indeed. I aspire to become a member of the *Club des Croqueurs de Chocolat*."

"The what?"

"The *Club des Croqueurs de Chocolat*. It is a famous organization based in France comprised of people who absolutely adore chocolate. I need two sponsors from within the organization, and I must complete a twelve-part questionnaire. It's a very difficult club to join, but that is my aspiration. I will be entertaining two gentlemen from France next month, both members of the *Club*. Tonight's tasting is sort of a dress rehearsal."

"I wish you success."

"*Merci*," he said. "The tasting is in my living room. Come on in."

His body swiveled on its axis as he led me into a room the size of the Astrodome. A long table covered with a white tablecloth somewhat reminiscent of the Last Supper filled the room. Unsalted crackers and bottles of Evian water were strategically placed within reach of each chair. Each place setting sported a nametag. My place at the table was next to a man named Mort Canard. He and his wife had not yet arrived.

"I would offer you a drink, but I don't want to damage your papillae," Pierre said.

"I understand," I said. I didn't, but at times one must make allowances.

Pierre disappeared into his kitchen, and I mingled with the other guests. My tablemate and his wife were the last to arrive.

"Got a drink, Pierre?" Mort asked.

"No!" Pierre rolled his eyes and returned to his kitchen. "No drinking before or during the tasting!"

Mort shrugged, grabbed his wife by the arm, and sulked. He was a tall man with rough hands, gray hair, a gray mustache, and scarlet skin stretched tightly over a strong jaw. His wife was thin and wore earrings that looked like the Leaning Tower of Pisa. Her funny face had a perpetual look of surprise, and her hair looked as if she had had it done in a wind tunnel.

"We've never met," Mort said to me. He looked at my name tag. "Winston Churchill?"

"Yes."

"I see," he said, but he didn't. "This is my wife, Daphne."

"How are you?" she asked. Her voice was thin, almost squeaky, and her eyes appeared to move in different directions as she spoke.

"I'm fine, thank you," I said. "I'm pleased to meet you."

"What do you do for a living?" Mort asked.

"I dabble," I said.

"Dabble, huh? Well, I'm Pierre's business partner, and I also own an investment house specializing in penny stocks. Quite a bit of money to be made in penny stocks."

"Yes, one penny at a time," Daphne laughed.

Mort glared at her with an impatience that he had cultivated over time, and then returned his attention to me.

"You should stop by and see me," he said. "I can make your money work hard for you."

"We can't have lazy money," Daphne giggled.

"Oh, shut up," Mort growled at her. "Well, Churchill, have you ever been to a chocolate tasting?"

"No, I haven't."

"Neither have I. Sounds silly to me. But that's Pierre. What's he going to do, serve us candy bars?" He laughed so hard I thought his tight skin would rip. It didn't.

"You may be pleasantly surprised," I said.

"I do have a sweet tooth," he stroked his chin.

"Many of them," his wife added.

Mort ignored her. Then Pierre reappeared with an army of assistants, and he drifted into the room as if he were on a silent chariot.

"Please, everyone take your seat," he said.

His assistants began placing large trays of chocolate on the table. Each piece of chocolate sat on a numbered card.

"This looks promising," I said.

"I'll reserve judgment," Mort replied.

"And I'll reserve a room at the inn," Daphne giggled. Mort shook his head and eyed the chocolate.

"Please eat the chocolate in numerical order," Pierre instructed. "That's very, very important. You must eat them in numerical order. I will guide you."

Mort immediately took a piece of chocolate from a card numbered '12', studied it, and plopped it into his mouth.

"Good lord!" he screamed. "What are you trying to do, Pierre, poison us? You call this bitter ash chocolate?" He deposited the partially eaten chocolate into his napkin.

Pierre glared at him.

"You stupid oaf!" he yelled at Mort. "You stupid, stupid oaf! You started with chocolate number twelve! Can't you follow directions? I told you to eat them in numerical order. You clearly know nothing about chocolate. You just spit out *Valrhona Guanaja 1502*, the finest chocolate in the world!"

"I suppose it's an acquired taste," I said.

"Acquired indeed," Pierre said. He looked at Mort. "One must have highly developed papillae to appreciate such fine chocolate."

I interpreted this to mean he thought Mort had no taste.

"Why would I want to acquire that putrid taste?" Mort growled.

Pierre crossed his arms and struck a defiant pose.

"People all around the world gladly pay top prices for that chocolate," he said. "People of good taste, that is."

"People pay for this?"

"Yes," Pierre said. "It's very expensive chocolate. Of course, appreciation for such fine chocolate cannot be bought at any price."

"So, people actually buy this?" Mort continued to stare at the chocolate in his napkin. The furrows in his forehead meant he was thinking.

"Now, if you would all pay attention to me and eat the chocolate **in order**." Pierre stared at Mort, but Mort wasn't paying attention. He was still thinking. As you will see, Mort was not the type of person you want to have thinking about any topic.

Pierre recovered his poise and conducted a very successful chocolate tasting. He watched over Mort the way a prison guard watches over Pubic Enemy #1. I dutifully consumed the chocolate in the correct order. By the time I had reached the *Valrhona Guanaja 1502*, my taste buds were sufficiently trained to handle the high cocoa content. I was rather proud of myself.

James arrived at the tasting's conclusion.

"Ah, James, did you find a place for the Rolls?" I asked.

"Yes, sir."

"Good. Unfortunately, the tasting is over."

He let only a little of his consternation show.

"Here," I handed him some chocolate. "I saved some of the world's finest for you."

"Very considerate, sir."

*   *   *

The fog lifted early on Telegraph Hill. I could have spent the entire morning comfortably stuffed into a cozy armchair admiring the views, but I didn't. No, I went shopping. Caroline Avalon's birthday was approaching, and fine chocolate from Pierre's shop seemed to be the perfect gift.

James prepared the Rolls, and we glided softly into the heart of San Francisco. Even in the city center, the fog was quickly dissolving into an azure sky, and The City's dampness began evaporating into the strengthening sunlight. James double-parked the Rolls in front of Pierre's shop on Union Square.

"I shall stay with the Rolls," he said. Good chauffeur, that James. One can never be too careful in San Francisco's perpetually gridlocked shopping mecca.

Two tall windows tastefully accented with gold and black trim flanked the entrance to Pierre's shop. I entered and strolled through the aisles of gourmet food items. The place appeared unmanned, but the store was logically arranged, and I quickly found some elegantly boxed chocolate that I knew Caroline would adore.

I pushed a button that I hoped would summon a clerk, but no such creature appeared. Instead, a commotion erupted in the back room.

"I will not do that!" It was Pierre.

"You will if you want to keep my financial backing!" It was Mort.

"What you're asking me to do is immoral!" Pierre screamed.

"What I'm asking you to do is good business," Mort countered.

"It's illegal to misrepresent a product!"

"It's only chocolate. Don't get so excited."

"You stupid oaf! You stupid, stupid oaf! It happens to be the finest chocolate in the world!"

"Listen, Pierre. If you want to stay in business, you'll do what I say. That's final."

"I will not ruin that chocolate." Pierre crossed his arms.

"Gentlemen," I said.

"Winston," Pierre jumped. "What are you doing here?"

"I came to buy some chocolate."

Pierre shot Mort a glance that would have felled a fox at fifteen hundred yards.

"You'd better do it now before this philistine forces me to degrade the world's finest chocolate."

Mort snickered. You could tell he would look up the meaning of the word "philistine" when he got home.

"What do you mean?" I asked.

"I'm leaving," Mort said. He pointed a nasty finger at Pierre's chest. "You just do what I told you to do, or you'll be out of business!" Mort turned and brushed past me.

Pierre was livid. He shook his fist at Mort.

"I'll get you for this, Mort Canard!" he screamed. "You'll never get away with it. You're a dead duck!"

Mort was unfazed. He waved goodbye with his back to us — very uncivilized behavior, in my opinion.

"Calm down, old sport," I said to Pierre. "What's going on?"

"Winston, that man is impossible. That uncultured savage wants me to dilute *Valrhona Guanaja 1502*. He wants me to melt it down, mix it with cheaper chocolate, repackage it, and still sell it as *Valrhona Guanaja 1502* at *Valrhona Guanaja 1502* prices. We'll make more money, but it's unthinkable! If anyone found out, I'd be ruined. And I'd never be admitted to the *Club des Croqueurs de Chocolat*. And the Frenchmen are arriving…" Pierre slapped his forehead.

"Then don't do it."

"You heard him. If I don't, he'll withdraw his financial backing."

"Can't you stay in business without him?"

"No. I guess I spend too much money pursuing my passions."

"Oh."

"Yes. It will just kill me if I have to ruin that fine chocolate. It's like painting over a Rembrandt."

"I'm sure it is."

"But what can I do?"

"I'm sure there's something," I shrugged. "Let me think about it."

"Will you?"

"Of course, I will."

I paid for Caroline's chocolate, not *Valrhona Guanaja 1502*, but not the cheap stuff, and returned to the Rolls. I explained Pierre's dilemma to James.

"Very unfortunate, sir."

"Yes, very unfortunate. James, I think we should learn a little more about Mr. Mort Canard."

"Yes, sir."

James drove us back to Telegraph Hill, and I dispatched him to see what he could dig up on Mort. The situation was clear: I had to persuade Mort to change his mind about diluting Pierre's precious chocolate or find a way for Pierre to raise enough money to buy out Mort's share of the business. Neither task would be easy. I opened a Bass Ale and decided to postpone any further thinking on the subject until James returned.

* * *

"Besides selling penny stocks, Mr. Canard is also involved in initial public offerings," James said. "They're called IPOs in the financial world. When a private company wants to go public and sell its stock, they arrange an IPO. Investment bankers like Mr. Canard find investors and set up the initial stock sale. Mr. Canard confines himself to low-priced IPOs - penny stocks. He has two offices: his main office in the heart of the Financial District and a branch office on the fringes."

"It's odd that he would have an office on the fringes, but there is nothing wrong with that," I said.

"No, there is not. However, the way Mr. Canard treats his clients is worrisome. After he arranges an IPO, he pressures the investors who initially purchased the stock to sell it back to him when it reaches some higher price. His branch office simultaneously pressures other clients into buying that same stock at an even higher price. Of course, these investors are unaware of this simultaneous buying and selling.

"For example, Client A buys a stock at $1.00 a share. Mr. Canard pressures them into selling the stock back to him when it reaches $1.50 a share. At the same time, his branch office pressures Client B into buying the same stock for $2.00 a share based on predictions that it will rise to $3.00 a share. Since it has already risen fifty cents a share in a very short time, it appears to be a good investment for Client B. Client B buys at $2.00 a share, and Mr. Canard makes a tidy fifty cents a share profit on the transaction."

"But what if the stock doesn't reach $1.50?"

"Through some clever manipulations, Mr. Canard ensures that it always does."

"Oh, I see. And the prediction that it will rise to $3.00?"

"Fabricated by Mr. Canard."

"Does it ever reach $3.00 a share?"

"Seldom."

"At least those who initially purchased the stock at $1.00 come out all right," I said. "They make fifty cents a share selling it back to Mort."

"Well, not exactly. Mr. Canard then pressures them into using their profits to invest in other stocks. They become the next victims, the next Client B."

"How unsporting."

"Very."

"But still, if we're talking of only pennies a share…"

"Do not be misled, sir. Often millions of shares trade hands. And then some people put their entire savings into penny stocks and end up with nothing."

"I get the point. Well done, James."

"Thank you, sir."

I sat back in my chair and took another sip of Bass Ale. The situation soon became very clear.

"James, I know how to get Pierre out of his chocolate mess."

"Very good, sir."

*   *   *

Do you remember Jacob Jepson? He was that pork chop eating, Cadillac driving, real estate scam chap that nearly stole the Duke's entire life savings. I remembered him well. And I was sure he would remember me. After what had happened in Nevada City, I had a hunch he wouldn't be too happy to see me. I was right. My hunches usually are. Fortunately, I James was with me.

"What are you doing here?" Jepson growled.

"Why aren't you mining gold in Nevada City?" I asked. I'll admit it wasn't the most tactful opening line.

He glared at me.

"I don't know where that prospector got his gold," he said. "But it wasn't from your land. You sold me a bill of goods and made me buy back the land I had already sold. And what for? Nothing. I should have sued you. In fact, I still might. You misrepresented that property."

"I didn't make you buy the land. You were greedy. And I don't think you'll sue me. You and Davidson were the first to misrepresent the land, and I don't think you're stupid enough to incriminate yourself."

Jepson took on the appearance of a furious monkey. James kept a close watch on him.

"What did you come here for?" Jepson asked. "Have some more land to sell?"

"This is no time for sarcasm, Jepson. No, no more land."

"Then why don't you leave. You've cost me enough money already."

"I have a way for you to get your money back."

"Ha! That's a laugh. You're the one who made me lose it in the first place!"

"Your greed made you lose it, not me."

"You cheated me."

"Like you had cheated the others. But let's let bygones be bygones. I can get your money back for you if you're interested."

"Why should I trust you? If you didn't have your goon with you, I'd toss you out of my office."

He looked at James. James raised his eyebrows but remained calm.

"Just listen to my idea. Being a businessman, even a crooked one, you'll appreciate it."

He stared at me.

"I think you should form another company," I said. "Form a company to mine the gold on your Nevada City property."

"There ain't no gold on that property!"

"You know that, and I know that, but no one else does."

"What are you talking about?"

"I know an investment banker in San Francisco who would arrange an initial public offering of your company's stock without asking any questions. His name is Mort Canard. Here's his card. When you get the money from the initial offering, you can leave the country like you were planning to after you sold that worthless land."

"I wasn't going to do that," Jepson snapped.

"Of course not," I smiled. "Now, what about this IPO?"

"You've got a big mouth. I shouldn't listen to a word you say." Jepson scratched his chin. He was thinking. He was mad, but he was thinking.

"You've got to admit; it's a good idea."

"Sounds plausible. If it were anybody but you, I'd probably go for it. How can I trust you? What are you getting out of this?"

"Satisfaction."

Jepson stared at me.

"What's your game?" he asked. "You get your kicks out of making people lose money?"

"I get my kicks out of justice," I said.

"Justice? There ain't no justice in this world."

"I'm offering you a chance to get your money back. That's justice. More justice than you deserve."

"I don't trust you. You're trying to play me for a fool again. Well, you won't do it this time."

"Listen, Jepson. You've got no money, just acres of worthless land. There's no reason for me to play you for a fool. You've got nothing to lose, and I can't make a cent off of you."

He looked at me for a long time. He was hungry and still greedy.

"It's a good scheme," he repeated. "I still don't trust you, but

I'll admit it's a good scheme."

"Just start a company," I said. "Make up some impressive records. You're good at that, and I'll take care of the rest. Oh, and insist on a firm underwriting from Canard. That will minimize your risk."

According to James, a "firm underwriting" represents a very high level of commitment from the investment banker. The banker uses his own money to buy the stock from the issuing company. If the IPO is a flop and the banker doesn't sell all the stock at the initial offering price, he's stuck with it and has to try to sell the shares at a lower price. All very bad for his profits. On the other hand, if the IPO takes off...

"I don't know," Jepson said. "You put a bad taste in my mouth."

"It's your choice. You can make some money, or you can stay broke. Once the lawsuits against Davidson Development and your other bogus companies are settled, you'll end up in jail unless you flee the country. Life abroad would certainly be more comfortable if you had some money."

Jepson's porcine face hardened. He pointed a steady finger at me.

"If you double-cross me this time, I'll kill you," he said.

* * *

I will admit that finance was becoming more exciting than I ever thought possible. It was rather sporting. I'm far from an expert in the field, but I'm a fast learner. James, it seems, knows considerably more.

Precisely twenty days after my visit to Jepson, I received a call from Mort. It takes twenty days for the Securities and Exchange Commission to approve a new stock issue. Mort was a real pro.

"Churchill, I have an opportunity for you," Mort said.

"You do?"

"Yes. I'm about to place an IPO for a company called Western Mineral Development. They mine precious metals, mainly gold. The initial price will be $5.00 a share, a little higher than I usually deal with, but I see it quickly hitting $10.00 a share. It's going to be a very hot stock. Are you interested?"

"It sounds risky," I said.

"Well, there's always a little risk. That's how big money is made. Of course, if you're not interested in big money…"

"I didn't say that."

"Good. Now, why don't you come by? I'm in my main office, and I'll be here all day."

"All right, I'll see you this afternoon."

"Good."

*　　　*　　　*

"Pierre, my friend, we're going to buy some stock," I slapped the old boy on the back.

"We are?" He looked at me as if he was wearing spectacles, but he wasn't.

"Yes."

"But I don't have any money," he said.

"Don't worry; I'll lend you some. You don't want to miss out on this investment."

"Really?"

"Yes. We will visit Mort this afternoon and invest in a new company called Western Mineral Development."

"Is it a solid investment?"

"It's worth its weight in gold," I said.

*　　　*　　　*

"Is that your Rolls Royce?" Mort asked, stretching his neck to see out of his ground-floor window.

James had just deposited us at Mort's main office. I've said it before, and you know I'll say it again: in my opinion, the 1963 Rolls Royce Silver Cloud III is the most beautiful motorcar in the world. What else would one drive to the Financial District?

"Yes," I said. "That's my Silver Cloud III."

Mort's jaw assumed a predatory pose.

"Very good," he said. It was only then that he noticed Pierre, and it gave him quite a shock. "Pierre, what are you doing here?"

"I hope you don't mind," I said. "But I told him about Western Mineral Development. He wants in on it too."

"Really?" Mort scratched his chin. His chin was still predatory but slightly softened. "Do you have any money to invest?" he said to Pierre.

"A little," Pierre said.

"Well," Mort clapped his hands together. "I'm glad both of you came to see me. I'll make it worth your while."

"I'm sure you will," I said. "How many shares are available?"

"Here's the prospectus." Mort handed me the preliminary description of the Western Mineral Development IPO. It was a fine piece of work. Jepson had outdone himself on this one.

"This is a red herring," I said.

Mort looked at me.

"You are a savvy investor, aren't you?" he said. His eyes turned into black marbles.

"What's a red herring?" Pierre asked. His eyes shot blanks and he blinked a lot.

"A red herring is a document that is given to potential investors before Securities and Exchange Commission approval," I said. "The catch is that it may contain incomplete information."

"Don't worry, Churchill. The final prospectus is identical to this one. I haven't had time to print a new version. You don't want to wait, do you? You'll have to act fast if you want to make big money on this one."

I pretended to study the red herring carefully.

"Let's see," I said. "Two hundred thousand shares are available."

"Yes," Mort said. "How many would you like?" His smile mimicked his jaw and became, you guessed it, predatory.

"One hundred thousand," I said.

Mort's body jerked backward as if an eel had crawled up his leg. He swallowed hard and loosened his tie.

"And I'll take twenty-five thousand," Pierre said. His mouth was so dry he could hardly speak.

"Twenty-five thousand?" Mort said. "That'll take a lot of money, Pierre. Where are you going to get it?"

I leaned over Mort's desk and spoke in a lowered voice.

"I'm giving him a bridge loan to cover the initial cost of his investment. If this stock's as hot as you say it is, Pierre will be able to pay me back without any problem. And I'll make a little bit of interest on the bridge loan." I winked at Mort.

"Churchill, I like your style," he smiled. "Of course, I will have to check your banking references, but if you own a Rolls Royce, I'm sure everything will be in order."

I smiled.

"Have you ever handled an IPO this big?" I asked.

"No, this is my biggest." There was a sudden resemblance between Mort and Jacob Jepson hunched over a pork chop.

"Do you have the resources to handle it?" I asked.

"Don't worry, Churchill. I know my business. Now let's celebrate our transaction with a drink."

$$* \qquad * \qquad *$$

Timing truly is everything in this world. Perfect execution depends on perfect timing. When it comes to high finance, one must know the proper time to buy and the proper time to sell. It also helps to be in the right place at the right time.

James took us back to Pierre's shop and then he immediately left for Mort's branch office.

"Where's James going?" Pierre asked.

"He's going to buy some stock."

"Why isn't he going to buy it from Mort?"

"He is."

Poor Pierre was confused. Finance wasn't his forte.

"But Mort's office is in the other direction. Where is he

going?"

"He's going to Mort's branch office."

Pierre's cheeks bulged in thought. He shook his head and went back to mixing a batch of chocolate. He tasted some and frowned.

"No good?" I asked.

"It's that diluted *Valrhona Guanaja 1502.*"

"You won't have to do that once this stock deal goes through," I said.

"I've got to be prepared if it doesn't. And the Frenchmen are arriving this afternoon. They're bound to find out what I'm doing. I'll be ruined, and my chances of joining the *Club* will be zilch."

"Would you like me to pick them up at the airport?" I asked. "A Rolls Royce always makes a good impression."

"Winston, that would be super!"

I tasted a small amount of his diluted chocolate.

"Awful, isn't it?" he said.

I nodded. It wasn't that bad.

"Can I have some?" I asked.

"If you really want it," he said. He looked at me oddly.

"I do."

He poured some chocolate into a mold, let it harden, wrapped it in foil, and placed it into a *Valrhona Guanaja 1502* package.

Then the telephone rang.

"Hello," Pierre answered. "Oh, it's you, Mort. Yes, Winston's here with me." He covered the receiver with his hand. "It's Mort," he said to me. "Things are happening with Western Mineral Development. The stock has just hit $7.10, and he wants us to sell it back to him."

"Tell him we'll sell when it hits $10.00," I smiled.

Pierre did as he was told and hung up.

"Now, what do we do?" Pierre asked.

"Wait."

"What for?"

"For the stock to hit $10.00."

"Do you think it will?"

"I'm positive."

"When?"

"Soon."

Mort called again ten minutes later. He asked to speak with me.

"I can't believe it, Churchill," Mort said. "Western Mineral is on fire. I've never seen anything like it. It just reached $9.00 a share, but I think you should sell now before everyone else begins to take profits. Don't take any chances. It's close enough to $10.00. Take your profit now."

"I suppose you're right," I said. "We'll sell."

"Good," Mort said. "You're making a good move. I'll repurchase the stock from you. You'll get your money quicker that way."

"What will you do with the stock?" I asked.

"I'll sell it to someone else," Mort said. "I may not be able to get $9.00 a share for it, but I'll make money off the commission. The important thing is for you and Pierre to take your profits."

"Yes, you're right," I said.

"Of course, we'll have to put your new profits to good use."

"I'm sure we'll find something."

"Yes, I'll help you find a good home for your money," Mort said. "I'll talk to you about it later. Goodbye, Churchill."

"Goodbye, Mort."

I hung up the phone and turned to Pierre.

"You now have one hundred thousand dollars, Pierre," I said. "Less the interest you owe me on your loan."

"What? I have how much?" The poor boy looked somewhat dazed. The weight of his lower lip pressed his jaw toward the floor.

"One hundred thousand," I said.

"A hundred thousand?" he mumbled. "I can't believe it. I have that much money?"

"Yes, but don't spend it yet. You're going to need it."

"I am?"

*   *   *

"James, is the Rolls ready? It's time to pick up the Frenchmen."

"Yes, sir."

Have you ever noticed how a Rolls Royce is allowed to double-park at airports? No, you probably haven't. Well, they are, and it's very impressive. James stayed with the Rolls while I went to greet our French visitors. You can always tell a Frenchman by the grandiose way in which he walks.

"Pierre Lupo sent me to greet you," I said to one of them.

The men looked at each other.

"That was very kind of heem," one of them said.

We shook hands like statesmen.

"My name is Winston Churchill," I said.

They looked at each other, muttered something in French, then turned toward me. I think they were a bit amazed.

"Weenston Churcheel?"

"No relation," I said.

"I am Claude Jambon."

"And my name is Georges Cochon."

"Pleased to meet you," I said.

They collected their luggage, and I led them outside. James

leaped into action and opened the rear door for them. They were quite impressed, and rightly so. My Rolls is impeccable, and James is a first-rate chauffeur.

"Beautiful automobeel," Claude said.

"Thank you," I beamed.

James smoothly placed the luggage into the boot and took his place behind the wheel. I sat in the front passenger seat - not a place I particularly care to be, but sometimes a gentleman must make sacrifices. Our guests were perfectly content in the luxurious back seat. They said something to each other in French that I didn't understand, but it seemed to be very complimentary.

James started the Rolls, and we effortlessly left the airport. I took out the chocolate Pierre had given me, unwrapped it, and put a piece into my mouth. The Frenchmen observed me, and they couldn't sit still.

"Would you like some chocolate?" I asked.

"But of course!" they said in unison.

I held out two pieces. They were wrapped in gold foil and covered with black paper with a red triangle in the lower-left corner.

"*Valrhona Guanaja 1502!*" Claude said, reading the label. "*Monsieur* Churcheel, your taste in chocolate is *tres bon.*"

"Thank you," I said.

Each of them took a piece and adroitly unwrapped it, cradling it like it was a newborn child. Claude sniffed his piece. Then he sniffed it again. A troubled looked crossed his face. Then he tasted it.

"*Monsieur* Churcheel, this is not *Valrhona Guanaja 1502!*"

Georges tasted his piece of chocolate and nodded so emphatically I thought his head would fall off. It didn't.

"Really?" I said.

"Where did you get this chocolate?" Claude demanded.

"From Pierre Lupo. Why, is something wrong?"

"Wrong? It is a crime to sell this, this," he pointed to the chocolate in his hand, "this dirt as *Valrhona Guanaja 1502*. We shall have stern words for *Monsieur* Lupo."

The two Frenchmen remained quiet with their arms folded for the remainder of the trip. James eased the Rolls to a stop in front of Pierre's shop and opened the rear door. The Frenchmen emerged and marched into the shop like stormtroopers. I followed.

"Gentlemen!" Pierre smiled. He offered his hand to them.

"What is the meaning of this?" Claude immediately demanded.

"What are you talking about?" Pierre asked. The poor boy was a bit stunned. It was not the greeting he had expected from the French delegation.

"This." Claude tossed the chocolate I had given him onto the counter.

Pierre looked at it and knew immediately what had happened.

"Winston, you gave them some of that chocolate!" he said.

"Sorry, old sport."

Suddenly, Mort Canard burst into the shop, and he looked like a man trying to avoid a runaway train.

"Pierre, how much money does the store have?" he asked.

Poor Pierre. Life was becoming far too complicated.

"Not much, really," Pierre answered. "Why?"

"I need money. Lots of it." Mort paced through the shop. The Frenchmen watched him as if he was a windup toy.

"What happened?" I asked.

"I've been had. That Western Mineral Development IPO was all a scam. It turns out there is no Western Mineral Development. It was a fake company. Those financial reports, everything."

"It's a good thing we sold," I said.

"Good for you, bad for me. After I bought the stock from you and Pierre, my other office sold it to another investor. That investor must have been part of the scam because his line of credit turned out to be phony. I found that out too late. Now I'm stuck owing you and Pierre the money for the shares I bought from you this morning. I also bought back shares from other people. Now I owe them, too. And I won't be receiving the money that I was supposed to receive from this other investor. The man behind Western Mineral Development has, of course, disappeared. So, I need money. Lots of it. This was the biggest deal I've ever done. I don't have the cash reserves to cover it. I'm ruined if I don't get some money."

"I'm sorry, Mort, but the shop account doesn't have much in it," Pierre said. "Maybe a couple of thousand at the most."

"That won't do. I'm ruined." The red skin over his jaw turned pale.

"Perhaps not," I said.

"What do you mean?" He perked up like a puppy expecting a good petting.

"I think perhaps we would be willing to exchange your share of this shop with the profits you owe us from the stock deal."

I looked at Pierre. Mort stared at us. Pierre blinked. Yes, the financial world can make one dizzy.

"I'd lose the tax breaks from this business if I sold it," Mort argued.

"You'll lose both businesses if you don't," I said.

Mort frowned and ran his fingers over his jaw. His skin returned to its natural red hue.

"Damn it, Winston, you're right," he said. "I don't have a choice. Would you really be willing to take my share of the shop?"

"What do you say, Pierre?" I asked.

Pierre nodded.

"Then it's a deal," Mort said. "I'll draw up the papers this evening, and we can sign them in the morning." Mort let out a deep breath and left the shop.

"Did you have something to do with all of this, Winston?" Pierre asked after he had recovered his senses.

"I may have had a hand in the affair," I said.

"What happened to that Western Mineral company?" Pierre asked.

"*Monsieur* Lupo," Claude interrupted. "What about this chocolate?"

"I can explain that," I said. "The man who just left was the shop's former owner, and he was responsible for this imitation *Valrhona Guanaja 1502*. Pierre discovered it and has just bought the shop from him in order to halt the sale of the imitation chocolate and preserve the purity and integrity of *Valrhona Guanaja 1502*."

Claude stepped back and raised his head.

"What a noble thing to have done," he said. He then gave Pierre three kisses on his cheeks. "There can be no question now of your becoming a member of *Le Club des Croqueurs de Chocolat*."

Pierre nearly fainted. I gave my regards to the Frenchmen and returned to the Rolls.

"Everything concluded satisfactorily, sir?" James asked.

"Indeed. I'd say everyone got their just desserts. Home, James."

10 THE ROGUE SAVES A TREE

The homes in San Francisco's Marina District have the finest views in the world, and the house I was staying in had them all. The San Francisco Bay, the Golden Gate Bridge, the yacht club. What more could one want? All right, so there may be a few other things, but not many.

The house's owners were away on an extended vacation, so I took the opportunity to make myself at home. Well, someone had to take advantage of those views.

*   *   *

The sky was overcast, and a blustery wind kicked up the waves and punched them back into the sea. The boats returning to the harbor bobbed on the water like giant corks. Occasionally, a blast of rain splattered against the window. It may not have been good sailing weather, but it was, all in all, good weather for contemplation.

I sipped a Bass Ale in front of a crackling fire and contemplated my invitation to a fundraiser sponsored by an environmental group I had never heard of. Now I'm as concerned about the environment as the next chap, but I have never shown a penchant for supporting any group of any kind. Still, a party is a party, and I suppose there was a chance that it would be as good as a post-opera bash. But not much of a chance.

James had my Rolls ready at precisely 7:30 PM, and we rolled off into the San Francisco night. The streets sparkled with rain, and automobile taillights reflected off the pavement like neon signs. The blustery wind that had shaken the waves now shook the traffic signals and blew bits of paper against the curb.

Our destination was the Portman Hotel, a ritzy hotel if one could call such sterility ritzy. It was all brilliant metal and sparkling glass, trendy furniture, and snooty staff. James glided my Rolls to the hotel's covered entrance. A doorman reached for my door, but James beat him to it, and the doorman retreated. Good chauffeur, that James.

Under-dressed, out-of-town guests huddled like mannequins in the lobby while they waited for transportation to take them to long-awaited engagements that could not possibly meet their expectations and would undoubtedly require embellishment when related to the folks back home. I shrugged and looked for a place to check my top hat, coat, and scarf. Yes, top hat. Fundraisers at expensive hotels demand top hats, white ties, and tails. Anything less would be positively uncivilized.

"Winston!" someone called from behind me.

I turned and was delighted to find not one of the mannequins but Greta Hutchins. Her formal attire was quite stunning, fitting for a fund-raiser at an expensive hotel. I must say that she looked much younger than her fifty-plus years.

"Greta," I took her hand and kissed her cheek. Have you ever noticed how a slinky, black Versace dress accented with elegantly simple gold jewelry can make any woman look as if she had just stepped out of a Jordan Playboy? If you have, then you move in the same circles as I do. If you have not, don't fret, I'll keep you informed.

There was no doubt that Greta looked like she had just stepped out of an elegant and sporty speedster. She had been a good friend of mine before she abruptly gave up a successful law practice and moved to the country. I recall her saying something about wanting peace of mind and solitude.

"My dear Winston," she said. "It's been such a long, long time."

"It certainly has."

We then experienced that pause that long-separated friends

experience when they attempt to reconstruct that something special that had made them friends in the first place. Don't worry; I'm not going to psychoanalyze it.

"You look like you're going to this fundraiser," I said.

"Going to it? My dear Winston, I'm throwing it!"

"Throwing it?" I am not easily startled, but I will admit that this was one of those rare occasions.

"Yes. Follow me. You shall be my date." She took me by the arm and led me into her party. She stopped after a few steps, took a step back, and looked at me.

"My dear Winston, how have you been?"

"I've been fine." I stepped back and looked at her Versace gown again. "You look terrific, and you look as if you've been doing well."

"It's rented," she laughed. "Hideous thing. You know this kind of costume is no longer me."

"Then you haven't given up the solitary country life?"

"No. Sorry to disappoint you."

"It's a relief, not a disappointment."

She then studied my tux.

"And I see you haven't changed. You always were the kind of man who dressed for the occasion."

I smiled. There was a time when that would have been the supreme compliment. These days I'm not so sure.

"Tell me about your fundraiser," I said.

"I will." She retook my arm, and we walked on. "I hope to raise a lot of money."

"That is typically the goal of a fundraiser."

We laughed.

"Who or what are you raising funds for?"

"Have you ever heard of a company called California Logging?"

"It sounds familiar, but it's not an institution I track on a daily basis."

"Someday, I'll ask you what institutions you do track on a daily basis. Anyway, they are the largest logging company in California. The business press refers to them as Cal Log. They're based in Mendocino County, where I've lived for the past ten years. Cal Log used to be one of the most responsible logging companies in the business, harvesting only as much timber as the forest could grow back. They treated their employees well, did not go into debt, and had lots of cash. They were true friends of their environment and community."

"What happened?"

"Because of their conservative logging policies, Wall Street felt they were not reaching their full profit potential. Naturally, their stock was undervalued. And with all of that cash sitting around, they were a perfect takeover target."

"Let me guess; they've been taken over."

"Yes, by a San Francisco man named Harold Buster. He's what the magazines refer to as a 'veteran takeover artist'. How would you like to be called that? Anyway, his purchase of Cal Log was typical of his style. He borrowed heavily through his holding company to finance the acquisition, and now he is selling Cal Log assets to pay off his debt. In this case, the assets are trees. Buster has accelerated the pace of logging to alarming proportions. He's mortgaging Mendocino County's future to pay off his debt, not to mention what he's doing to the environment. That is unacceptable, Winston, and he must be stopped. I've formed an organization to stop him, and I'm throwing this party to raise money to save the trees."

"A worthy endeavor," I said.

"I knew you would think so. We have filed lawsuits against Cal Log, but of course, lawsuits take time. Too much time I'm afraid. And money, way too much money."

"There must be other ways."

"Yes, there are other ways, but they would require a man of extraordinary ability." She gave me that film screen femme fatale look. "It would require a man like you."

"Cut the ticker-tape parade, baby," I said.

"All right, I'll get to the point. I've known all along that unorthodox methods would have to be employed to stop Harold

Buster. Of course, I thought of you immediately. I've heard about your adventures in Latin America and a few other escapades here in the Bay Area. You never could turn down a good cause, could you? Now I'm asking you to join another one. Will you help me?"

"I was wondering how I had gotten invited to this affair," I smiled.

"You're not the only clever person in this world, Winston Churchill." Her smile would have made Lauren Bacall jealous. "Will you help me?"

In case you don't know, I'm a hopeless romantic, always compelled to come to the aid of a damsel in distress.

"Of course, I will," I sighed.

She smiled like a cat who had just eaten the family parakeet.

"Good, I knew I could count on you."

"Now tell me about this Harold Buster fellow."

"He's an ass."

That was Greta, all right, direct, and to the point.

"I'm sorry, Winston, but he is."

"No apology necessary. I would, however, like to know more about his business affairs."

"Yes, of course. I have a file in my car, and you can have it after the party. Now I must mingle and raise some cash — you may need it." Greta kissed me on the cheek and went to work on her quests.

I roamed the room searching for someone I knew, but all of the guests were strangers to me. This wasn't the kind of party that acquaintances of mine would attend. Pity. I could lecture you on the importance of supporting worthy causes, but I'll spare you. The next time you may not be so lucky. When the crowd thinned, Greta reappeared at my side.

"How did you do?" I asked.

"As well as could be expected. Everyone claims they want to protect the environment, but when it comes to putting their money where their mouth is, well…"

"Yes, I can imagine. And I'm sure Buster has a few friends in this town that would like to see you fail and who would discourage contributions to your cause."

"He also has a few enemies who would like to see me succeed. A few of them wrote checks on the spot. Others committed to sending their money. We'll see about that."

I smiled.

"Come on; I'll give you my file on Harold Buster."

She took me by the arm and led me out of the hotel to a beat-up VW bus. That was more her style. The vehicle's two-tone white on dark orange paint scheme reminded me of an ice cream cone.

"Excuse the mess," she said, opening the side door. "This is a work vehicle."

A work vehicle, indeed! It was filthy! Imagine the scope of the tragedy if the seats had been covered with Connolly hides. In my opinion, the soiling of Connolly hides is a crime and one that should be dealt with severely. But you didn't ask for my opinion, did you?

Greta shuffled through a pile of boxes and removed a thickly stuffed file folder. She considerately wiped the dust off of it before handing it to me. A classy gesture on her part.

"Here is everything I know about Harold Buster," she said. "You can probably learn more if you happen to know a good stock analyst. Public information will not be hard to find. Private information will, of course, be harder."

"And more useful," I winked.

"Call me if you come up with anything," she said.

"Where are you staying?"

"At some fleabag hotel down the road. I'll give you the number."

"Fleabag hotel?" I said. "We can't have that. I'm staying in a large house on the Marina, and there's enough room for both of us."

"I should have suspected," she said. She gave me a sly, film noir grin.

"Leave your bus here. James will take us."

On cue, James drove up to the curb in my Rolls. Greta looked at it and grinned.

"Winston Churchill, you always did have class," she said.

*   *   *

Greta rose late the next morning. I had already spent several hours studying her Harold Buster file.

"You get up early," she said, dragging herself across the room to my desk. Then she looked out the window. "My God, what a view!"

"Yes, I rather like it. A good view is not to be wasted."

"Don't you find it distracting? I think it would take my mind off work."

"Not my mind. I find it peaceful. Helps me think. James can get you some coffee if you'd like."

"Yes, I'd like that." She pulled up a chair and sat down. She had that dreamy look on her face.

"Tell me," I said. "Isn't it lonely up there in Mendocino?"

My words ignited a fireworks display of surprise in her face.

"What do you mean?"

I looked at her the way a trainer looks at a young thoroughbred whose first training session was quick enough to win the Derby.

"Well, a little," she frowned. "But I do a lot of fishing. I've always loved fishing, and now I have the time to do it. And I've got my books. And there's always something to do around the house."

I continued to look at her.

"My dear Winston," she shook her head. "You always could see right through me. Yes, at times, I am lonely. But I choose to be. Now, tell me what you think of Harold Buster."

"Changing the subject won't help," I said. "But I'll let you off the hook." I turned my attention to the papers scattered on the desk. "The name of his holding company is a bit pretentious."

"Top Group," she giggled. "You don't get to Harold Buster's position without being a little pretentious."

"I suppose not."

"What else is interesting?" she asked.

"Everything appears to be fairly typical. At the time Buster made his offer of $32 a share, he, through Top Group, already owned 26% of Cal Log's total stock. Lucky for him that he didn't own more than that. Thirty percent ownership would have triggered an anti-takeover provision. Owning less than thirty percent gave him time to arrange his financing without revealing his intentions. As it was, he ended up paying $39 a share. He financed the purchase through junk bonds underwritten by the investment banking firm of Hamler Brothers. That gave him $900 million in additional debt. He's paying off that debt by cutting down and selling trees at a staggering pace. That, I presume, is where you come in."

"Precisely. We must stop him before he destroys all the forests in Northern California."

"He won't be easy to stop. He hasn't done anything illegal that I can see."

"On the surface, it all looks kosher, but there are always skeletons in the closet when something like this happens. Even if his deal is legitimate, we must stop him." She turned away and stared out of the window. Her gaze crossed the bay and went all the way to the forests of Mendocino.

"Have you talked to him about this?" I asked.

"I tried to, but he sent his lawyers after me. I didn't even get a foot in the door."

"Not very hospitable."

"I told you he's an ass."

"Yes, well, I need to know a little more about him other than his being an ass." I turned my attention back to the file. "If you're going to topple someone like Buster, you have to know what makes him tick."

"He collects books," Greta said.

"What?"

"That was my reaction, too. It doesn't seem like the kind of hobby he would have, does it?"

"It does if you think about it."

She thought about it.

"Yes, you're right," she flashed me a knowing grin.

"So, Harold Buster collects books," I said after a short pause. "You're quite the bookworm, too, aren't you?"

"I've always had an appreciation for fine books, if that's what you mean." Her words were as biting as an immature whiskey.

"Well, well, you and Harold Buster have something in common," I teased.

"We have nothing in common," she snapped. "The man is an ass. We must stop him!" She turned her back to the window.

"Don't worry; I'll dispatch James. If there are any skeletons in Harold Buster's closet, he will find them."

"Who is this James?" she asked.

"He's my chauffeur."

*   *   *

"Jenkins McCoy?" I asked. "Who is Jenkins McCoy?"

James stood before me with an open notebook.

"A shady character. No one seems to know him well. I am told he is a close friend of Sid Hamler," he said.

"Of Hamler Brothers?"

"Yes, sir. Actually, Sid Hamler is the only Hamler at Hamler Brothers. I am told Mr. Hamler thinks Hamler Brothers sounds more important than simply Hamler."

"I suppose it does. And two days before Buster made his offer, Jenkins McCoy purchased 250,000 shares of Cal Log?"

"Correct."

I looked at Greta.

"Looks as if someone gave him a hot tip," I said to her.

"It sure does," she said. "Of course, it's all circumstantial."

"You're right. We have no evidence of a crime."

"And we need hard evidence," Greta said. She rose and paced across the room.

"Still, it gives me a good enough reason to continue investigating the Hamler-Buster connection," I said. "Sid Hamler's records might be interesting."

"Yes, they might prove insider trading or something like that," Greta said.

"Quite possibly. James, any ideas?"

"Yes, sir." He closed his notebook. "I think we should obtain Mr. Hamler's records. All of his records."

"Excellent idea!" I said.

"Thank you, sir."

"Well, then. Have at it."

"What's he going to do?" Greta asked.

I smiled, and James nodded and departed.

"If there is anything to be found, James will find it."

"Who is this James?" Greta asked.

*   *   *

We waited for James at the Petit Cafe, a nice little neighborhood restaurant away from the more bustling parts of The City. We settled down at a cozy table in front of a large window and enjoyed a fine lunch.

"What will you do if James finds something?" Greta asked.

I shrugged. A slice of French bread topped with brie, roasted peppers, olive oil, and garlic occupied my attention.

"You know, once one tastes seventy percent brie, one never settles for sixty," I said.

"What does that have to do with Harold Buster?"

"Nothing."

"I see," she said, but she didn't.

"One must always maintain one's civility even while pursuing a formidable villain."

"Winston Churchill, you are the most singular man I have ever known, " Greta laughed.

"Is that a compliment?"

"Sometimes." Her femme fatale look returned.

"I suppose this means you want to resume talking business."

"I'm sorry, but do you think there is something we can do to stop Buster?"

"If a crime has been committed, justice must be served," I said.

"What if a crime has not been committed?"

"That's harder. Now eat your brie and enjoy the wine."

Greta smiled and did as I suggested. We had just ordered dessert when James floated my beautiful Rolls to a rest in front of the restaurant.

"Here's James now," Greta said, jumping up from the table. The girl was a bit excited.

James emerged from the Rolls with a large file folder under his arm.

"Looks like he's found something," she ran to the door.

"You can always count on James."

"Who is he?" she looked back at me.

James entered the restaurant, and she escorted him to our table.

"James, have a seat," I said.

"Thank you, sir." He sat down and placed the folder in front of me.

"What have we here?"

"Information, sir."

I smiled and opened the folder. I did not need to go beyond the first page. A nearly invisible grin crossed James' face.

"What?" Greta asked. "What is it?"

"At the time of Buster's offer to purchase Cal Log, Hamler Brothers, Buster's investment banker, secretly owned 25% of Cal Log stock. Hamler had masked his stock purchase through several holding companies controlled by Jenkins McCoy."

"So?"

I quickly put twenty-six and twenty-five together.

"That means between them, Buster and Hamler owned 51% of Cal Log."

"So?"

"Thirty percent ownership would have triggered the anti-takeover provision that would have virtually prevented anyone from acquiring the company."

"How so?" Greta asked.

"Before any single investor could acquire over 30% of Cal Log stock, the purchase had to be approved by a majority of Cal Log shareholders. Buster was Hamler's client. Together they owned 51% of Cal Log stock, a majority and enough to guarantee approval of Buster's purchase of more stock, enough stock to control the company. Buster and Hamler must have been secretly working together, and that's how they engineered the takeover of Cal Log. And the 250,000 shares Jenkins McCoy purchased must have been his payoff for running the holding companies Hamler used to shield his holdings."

"Winston, what are you going to do?" Greta asked.

"Throw the book at him."

* * *

George Thomason, a London bookseller, collected 23,000 books and pamphlets published in England during the troubled years of conflict from 1640 to 1661 to preserve them for posterity. I know this because I researched the subject. Book collecting that is. A man's passion can also be his weakness.

"Oh, you're a book collector?" the administrative voice at the other end of the phone said. "Then I'm sure Mr. Buster will have time for you. What was it you said you had?" As I had suspected, the way to Harold Buster's heart was through his books.

"A collection of Shakespeare once owned by Henry Clay Folger," I said.

"Just a minute." She put me on hold. A minute and fifty-three seconds later, she was back on the line. "Yes, Mr. Buster will be glad to meet you. Shall we say two o'clock this afternoon?"

"Let's say two-thirty." An extra half-hour of anticipation never hurt anyone.

"Two-thirty it is, mister, ah, what did you say your name was?"

"My name is Winston Churchill."

"Is it really?" There was a smile in her voice.

"Yes, but no relation."

"Oh."

At two-thirty, I was in the heart of the Financial District. Even in San Francisco's money mecca, a 1963 Rolls Royce Silver Cloud III attracts attention, particularly one as well-maintained as mine. I must say I was well-maintained, as well, snappily attired in a gray, double-breasted suit, an azure tie, pocket square, and impeccably polished, black oxford shoes. Today, I meant business.

James eased the Rolls to a halt in front of 460 Montgomery Street. Buster's office was on the twenty-fifth floor. The elevator took me there in silence. Not even the doors made a sound as they opened. The hallway was hushed, like an empty church at two o'clock on a Tuesday afternoon. Have you ever wondered how they make modern office buildings absorb so much sound? Maybe you haven't. Well, I have, and I find it unsettling.

I located the Top Group offices and found Buster's secretary sitting behind an expansive, dark desk.

"Hello, I'm Jenny McCoy-Barrett, Mr. Buster's personal secretary. She was dressed, well-dressed, I might add, in a solid black, Ralph Lauren dress that made her look more like a CEO than a secretary.

"Ralph Lauren?" I asked her.

"Why, yes. How did you know?"

"I know these things."

She studied my attire, and her face lightened with mild admiration.

"Yes, you look as if you would."

She led me into an office with a panoramic view of the city. Pictures of fishermen up to their hips in water adorned the walls.

"Mr. Churchill, I presume." A delicate man stood behind a sturdy desk and held out his hand.

"Yes." I shook his hand.

"I am Harold Buster." His face radiated enthusiasm. He did not look at all as I had expected him to. I had expected a slightly overweight torso, balding egg-shaped head, and the demeanor of a piranha. What stood before me was a man with a thin, long face and black curly hair cut short and firmly in place. Eyeglasses with perfectly round lenses clung to the bridge of a small, sharply defined nose. He must have been in his early fifties, although he looked much younger at first glance. And, he wore a bespoke suit – a nice charcoal pinhead from Henry Poole of London. Quite impeccable. A man with such refined sartorial taste deserves some respect, even if he plays loose with financial rules.

"I always enjoy meeting fellow book collectors," he said. "Please sit down."

I did. The leather chair was comfortably stuffed.

"Are you a fisherman?" I asked, nodding at the pictures on the wall.

"Why, yes," he smiled. "Next to book collecting, fishing is my greatest passion. But please tell me about these books. I've been thinking about them all day and haven't been able to get a bit of work done."

"I have a collection of Shakespeare once owned by Henry Clay Folger. The books are filled with his annotations."

His eyes brightened. A book annotated or marked by a prominent owner is particularly desirable to some collectors.

"Really?" he said. "My collection is modest, but I specialize in books once owned by the great financial tycoons. Henry Huntington, J. Pierpont Morgan, those people. Most of their books are either in museums or the libraries they founded. One rarely encounters one that isn't."

"That's what makes this Shakespeare collection so valuable."

"Yes, Mr. Churchill, it is indeed valuable. You must be interested in selling the collection; otherwise, you wouldn't have come to see me."

"You are correct. The books have fallen into the hands of an acquaintance of mine. She is not a collector and therefore wants to sell them. Myself, I collect only the works of Fitzgerald. Since they do not fit into my collection, I agreed to help her find a buyer. I have no interest in them apart from appreciating their value as rare books."

"I see. Well, I am interested. When can I see them?"

"We could show them to you tonight."

"Excellent! Why don't you come to my home? Then I can also show you my collection."

"Very good."

"Here's the address." He used a Mont Blanc Meisterstück pen to scribble his address on a piece of thick writing paper.

I rose to leave.

"Your wife?" I asked, looking at the picture of a woman on his desk.

"My late wife," I said.

"Oh, I'm sorry."

"That's all right. She was a good woman. I've never remarried. Books and fishing fill my time now."

I turned to leave, then stopped.

"Oh, there is something I'm curious about," I said.

"What is it?"

"Didn't you recently purchase California Logging?"

"Yes, why?" His face soured.

"I read about it in the papers."

"Don't believe everything you read in the papers. I'm getting a bum rap. They say I'm depleting the forests. Nonsense. There's enough timber up there to last us in perpetuity. I've also put in $12 million of my own money to build a new power plant up there. I'm in it for the long haul, contrary to what the press says."

"It has been a messy fight, though, hasn't it?"

"Messy? I'll tell you how messy. Those environmentalists are putting large metal spikes into the trees. The spikes are meant to destroy saw blades, but they also injure saw operators. I like a good fight as much as the next man, but fair is fair."

"I didn't know about the spikes."

"No, no one does. The press doesn't print that sort of thing."

"There is one more thing I'm curious about," I said.

"What's that?"

"Jenkins McCoy purchased 250,000 shares of Cal Log just before you made an offer for it."

"Who's Jenkins McCoy?" Buster asked.

"You don't know who he is?"

"No."

"You do know Hamler Brothers, don't you?"

"Yes. They're my investment bankers."

"When you made your offer for Cal Log, Hamler Brothers owned 25% of Cal Log stock. You owned 26%. Together you owned enough to control the company but not enough individually to trigger the poison pill."

"What do you mean Hamler Brothers owned 25% of Cal Log?" I almost believed his surprise.

"I suppose you didn't know that, either?"

"No, I didn't."

"I find that surprising," I said.

"So do I." Buster lost himself in his thoughts. I must say he had a way of oozing sincerity. Perhaps it was the bespoke suit. But I've been around enough of these high-finance types to be wary of any outward display of emotion, no matter how convincing. Acting must be part of every major business school's curriculum.

"I suppose you read that in the newspapers, too," Buster said.

I shrugged and decided to drop my pursuit of the truth for now. I knew I could count on James to dig up the real dirt.

"Well, Mr. Buster, fortunately for book collectors such as ourselves, printing presses have been used to print things other than newspapers."

Buster regained his smile.

"You're right, Mr. Churchill," he said. "I'm looking forward to seeing you this evening."

"It will be my pleasure," I said.

We shook hands, and I left.

*   *   *

"James," I said. "I think we may have to change our approach to Harold Buster."

"Sir?"

"There are always two sides to every story. I have just heard the other side of the Cal Log story, and it is an interesting one. I believe further research is in order."

"Yes, sir."

*   *   *

"These are fabulous," Greta said, carefully browsing through the Shakespeare editions. "Where did you get them?"

"Never mind," I said.

She gave me the kind of glance an experienced investor gives to a neophyte with a hot stock tip.

"All right, I don't want to know."

"All you need to know is that Harold Buster will pay a lot of money for those books," I said. "You can sell them to him and use the money in your efforts to defeat him."

"Wonderfully ironic," she smiled.

"I knew you would appreciate it. By the way, we're going to his home tonight to show him the books."

"What?" Her smile dissolved like sugar into a hot cup of espresso.

"We're taking the books to him. I told Buster they belonged to an acquaintance of mine. You are that acquaintance."

"But Winston, I despise that man!"

"You've been trying to see him. Here's your chance."

She frowned.

"You can pull it off," I said. "You like books."

"I used to like books. Now I like fishing."

"So does Harold Buster."

"He does?"

"Yes," I said. "Next to book collecting, fishing is his greatest passion. You see, you two have a lot in common."

She gave me a nasty look.

"We have nothing in common," she growled. "The man is an ass!"

*　　*　　*

Harold Buster's home was in San Francisco's Cow Hollow neighborhood, an area full of finely manicured manors. His house was a splendid structure neighboring a foreign embassy. James glided the Rolls to a halt in the driveway. We were high above the bay, above the trees and buildings, closer to the stars than the ocean. The lights of Marin County glittered across the bay.

James rang the doorbell.

"We shall soon see how much you and Buster truly have in

261

common," I said to Greta.

"Winston! Don't tease me!"

"Relax," I said. "You're about to slay your enemy with his own sword."

Buster opened the door himself. He held it open and motioned us inside.

"Mr. Churchill, I'm glad to see you again," he said. He shook my hand.

I glanced at Greta. She, too, was surprised by Buster's physical appearance.

"This is my acquaintance, Greta," I said.

"Pleased to meet you," Buster said.

He looked at her and smiled. Greta nodded demurely.

"Are those the books?" Buster pointed at the bundle under James' arms.

"Yes," Greta said.

She took a book from James and handed it to Buster. He opened it and flipped through the pages.

"This is fantastic!" he said.

The words in the book took him to a different world, and we followed him into it. We arrived at his library; it was a spacious room larger than many bookstores. The walls were covered with dark wood bookcases filled with real books. A fire blazed in a Victorian fireplace surrounded by two sumptuous leather wingback chairs. A large antique wood table occupied the center of the library. All in all, the room was stunning enough to be the subject of a feature article in an architectural magazine. James put the remaining volumes of Shakespeare on the table and quietly left the room.

"Please, sit down," Buster said to Greta.

She sat in one of the chairs by the fire; Buster sat in the other. I stood by the table. Buster could not take his nose out of the Shakespeare. He sifted through the pages for several minutes before speaking again.

"Greta, this book is exquisite," he said. He pulled his chair closer to hers.

"Yes, it is," she said. She successfully overcame the urge to pull away.

"Look at the condition of the pages," he held the book up for her to see. "They're almost in original condition."

"How can you tell?" she asked.

"Feel how smooth they are."

She ran her fingers over the page.

"And very little discoloration," Buster said. "Only a little around the edges."

Greta looked closer.

"Yes, I see," she said.

"You say these once belonged to Henry Clay Folger?" Buster

asked.

"Yes," I answered.

"They're filled with his inscriptions," Greta said. "I was reading them before we arrived."

"Really?"

"Yes," Greta said. "Look." She took the book from Buster and thumbed through the pages until she found writing in the margins.

"Marvelous," Buster said.

"Read it," Greta suggested.

Buster read it and laughed.

"Incredible!" he said. "He must have used that in a speech. That's why I love annotated books. Not only are they more valued by collectors, but they also reveal things about their previous owners."

"That does make them more interesting." Greta couldn't suppress a smile. She tried, she tried very hard. But she couldn't do it.

Have you ever noticed how lusciously mellow a *Chateau Certan de May* becomes as it breathes? Perhaps you haven't. Trust me, it does. And that's exactly what was happening with Greta. Buster's infectious enthusiasm had uncorked her softer nature, and she was doing a fine job of forgetting that he was the ogre who owned Cal Log.

"Winston may not have told you," he said. "But I only collect books that have been previously owned by famous financial tycoons. Few of the books I have are annotated. I don't think many of those old tycoons read anything but ticker tapes. That's why I find this collection so exciting."

"They are magnificent volumes," Greta agreed.

They browsed through the other books for quite some time and shared their opinions on the annotations.

"Mr. Churchill told me you enjoy fishing," Buster said after they had been through all of the books.

"He did?" She turned and looked at me.

I smiled.

"Yes," Buster said. "I also enjoy fishing."

"You do?"

"Yes. I go whenever I can. I'm almost as fanatical about fishing as I am about books. Winston may have told you about all of the fishing pictures I have hanging on my office walls." He kind of blushed.

"No, he didn't," Greta said. She turned and looked at me again.

"I find that fishing cleanses the mind, don't you?" Buster said.

"Yes, yes, I do," Greta agreed.

"Where do you fish?" Buster asked.

"Streams and rivers," Greta answered. "I prefer them to the

ocean."

"You do? That's wonderful! So do I."

"Really?" Greta asked.

"Yes!"

They exchanged fish stories for half-hour and acted like old chums. I wasn't too surprised.

"Where do you fish?" Buster asked.

"In Mendocino County."

"That's terrific! I have business interests up there. Perhaps we could fish together sometime."

Greta suddenly tightened.

"Cal Log," she said grimly.

"Yes, how did you know?"

"I know all about you and what you're doing. You're destroying the forests."

Buster reacted the way a horse reacts to a rattlesnake. His skin turned red.

"Don't believe what you read in the papers," he said. "I am not destroying the forests."

"Yes, you are, and I will stop you!" Greta rose and stared at her adversary.

"What?" Poor Buster was stunned and confused. Greta's words had rocked him like a prizefighter's left jab.

"I tried to see you once, but your lawyers ran me off. Now I'm taking action."

"Who are you?" Buster asked.

"Greta Hutchins."

"Oh." Buster deflated.

"You're destroying Mendocino County to pay off your company's debt."

"Listen here; you people are no angels. Don't you know that those spikes you put into the trees hurt the loggers? I may hurt trees, but I don't hurt people."

Greta blushed.

"You're mortgaging the future of Mendocino County," she countered. "You'll take the trees and run." She took a piece of paper from her pocket. "Look at this proxy statement," she shook the statement in front of his face. "It says Cal Log could consider selling additional timberlands in the future if it provides greater returns than holding and harvesting them or if Cal Log is required to raise cash. All of that debt you've piled onto Cal Log makes it very likely that you'll have to raise cash to make the loan payments. Then there go the forests, there go the jobs, and there goes Mendocino County."

"Listen, I'm building a new power plant up there with my own money," Buster countered. "I wouldn't be doing that if I wasn't in it for the long haul."

"Until it's more economical to be in it for the short-haul. And what about the way you acquired Cal Log?"

"I acquired it fair and square!"

"Ha! You and Sid Hamler conspired to avoid the anti-takeover provision."

"I did not!"

They fell silent and stared at each other.

"Ahem," I interrupted. "I believe this may be the appropriate time to inform you that James has discovered some additional information that may expedite your reconciliation."

Buster and Greta looked at me, then each other, then at James, who had quietly re-entered the room.

"Enlighten us, James," I said.

"Yes, sir. Mr. Buster, did you ever wonder why your takeover of Cal Log went so smoothly?"

"I assumed it was because I had good investment bankers." He turned to Greta, then to me, then back to James.

"It went so smoothly because an anti-takeover provision was cleverly circumvented."

The glare returned to Greta's eyes. Her initial distrust of Buster reappeared like wild weeds after a rainstorm.

"How did that happen?" Buster asked.

"Yes, how did that happen," Greta sarcastically asked.

"Your investment banker, Hamler Brothers, colluded with a certain Jenkins McCoy to secretly accumulate enough stock to control the company but fly under the radar of the anti-takeover provisions. You benefitted from that maneuver."

"Is that the Jenkins McCoy you told me about, Winston?" Buster asked.

Greta was on the verge of igniting him with torrents of flaming anger.

"That was our question, too," James continued.

Buster turned to Greta, hoping to find a morsel of support. He found none.

"Well, what did you find?" Buster asked.

"I discovered that Jenkins McCoy does not exist."

Greta nearly exploded. All of this was evidence enough to justify her original perception of Buster.

"What?"

"I have discovered that Jenkins McCoy is actually Jenny McCoy-Barrett."

"Jenny McCoy-Barrett? That's my secretary!" Buster jumped.

"Yes, sir."

Buster's eyes widened until they became the size of his open mouth.

"She was using information stolen from your office to work some very lucrative deals with Sid Hamler," I said.

"Very illegal lucrative deals," James added.

"What? I can't believe this." Buster shook his head like a dog shaking off water.

"Winston, is this true?" Greta asked.

"All of it. We have indisputable proof."

Buster sat down. The poor boy looked like a racecar driver who had run out of fuel within sight of the finish line.

"And Harold knew nothing of this?" Greta asked.

"Nothing," I said.

"I shall have to make amends," Buster whispered to himself.

Greta was genuinely moved. Tiny tears may have formed in the corners of her eyes, or it may have simply been the light. Before I could determine which, Buster pulled himself together and sat upright.

"Look," Buster said to Greta. "Before the subject of Cal Log came up, we were having a grand time talking about books and fishing. I felt as if I had known you for years. We do have a lot in common. We may have some misunderstandings about Cal Log…"

"We most certainly do." Greta buttoned her lips and crossed her arms.

"But I think we can resolve those differences," Buster continued. "I understand the situation better now, don't you?"

Greta stared at him for a long time.

"Maybe I do," she finally said.

"See, understanding is the first step. I'm sure we can come to some agreements."

"I don't know," Greta said. "Perhaps we can." She uncrossed her arms.

"You were having fun, too, weren't you?" Buster asked.

"Yes, yes I was." She tried to hold back the words, but they cascaded from her mouth like water over Niagara Falls.

"There! Let's keep our minds open and work out our differences. After all, we're both fishermen."

"You may have a point," Greta said. She spoke again after a long pause. "Maybe we can come to some agreement."

"Let's start by agreeing to dinner together."

Greta hesitated, but I knew her well enough to know she would agree.

"I suppose it wouldn't hurt," she said.

"Good!" Buster smiled.

Greta turned to me.

"You knew this would happen, didn't you?" she said.

I raised my eyebrows.

"You arranged the whole thing," she said. "You somehow knew Harold, and I would hit it off."

"Haven't I been telling you that you two have a lot in common?" I said. "Now, I will gracefully withdraw and leave you to deal with Harold Buster. You no longer require my assistance."

"My dear Winston." She came to me, looked me in the eyes,

smiled, and kissed me on the lips. "You are a sly one."

I smiled and followed James to the Rolls.

"I trust that the trees have been saved, sir?" James asked.

"Yes, they have. All's well that ends well. Home, James."

The End

ABOUT THE AUTHOR

David Biagini grew up in a small Illinois town playing Clue and reading the Hardy Boys Mysteries (the Hardy Boys Detective Handbook still sits on his bookshelf). With no real crimes to solve, he wrote his own with a writing style that combines Raymond Chandler's sharp similes with P. G Wodehouse's sly wit.

He received a Bachelor of Arts degree in English Literature from Northern Illinois University and then moved to California, where he conceived The Lovable Rogue Mysteries. He currently lives in a remote New Mexico outpost.

When not writing mysteries, he composes music and makes films; his music videos have enjoyed success in international and domestic film festivals.

For news about The Lovable Rogue Mysteries and blogs combining mysteries and fashion, visit https://www.thelovablerogue.com.

Other books by David Biagini

The Polo Mallet Murders
ISBN: 979-8621985691

Murder Is The New Black
ISBN: 979-8583085842

Clothes Make The Corpse
ISBN: 979-8363414305

Made in the USA
Coppell, TX
22 April 2023

15947327R00163